The Rags of Time

NOVELS BY

BARBARA GOOLDEN

Call the Tune
The Asses' Bridge
Crown of Life
'The Best Laid Schemes . . .'
Men as Trees
Swings and Roundabouts
Community Singing
Ichabod
Daughters of Earth
Jigsaw
From the Sublime to the
    Ridiculous
Strange Strife
Venetia
The China Pig
Truth is Fallen in the Street
Return Journey
Who is my Neighbour?
The World his Oyster
Bread to the Wise
At the Foot of the Hills
The Singing and the Gold
To Have and to Hold
The Nettle and the Flower
Through the Sword Gates
The Linnet in the Cage
Sweet Fields
The Ships of Youth
A Pilgrim and his Pack
Where Love Is
For Richer for Poorer
New Wine
Falling in Love
One Autumn Face
Against the Grain
To Love and to Cherish

The Pebble in the Pond
The Little City
Battledore and Shuttlecock
Love-in-a-Mist
Marriages are Made in Heaven
The Gentle Heart
The Gift
Fool's Paradise
Blight on the Blossom
A Finger in the Pie
The Lesser Love
Nobody's Business
Anvil of Youth
A Time to Love
Second Fiddle
A Time to Build
The Eleventh Hour
All to Love
The Reluctant Wife
A Marriage of Convenience
Today Belongs to Us
The Snare
A Question of Conscience
Fortune's Favourite
No Meeting-Place
Before the Flame is Lit
A Leap in the Dark
A Law for Lovers
Time to Turn Back
The Broken Arc
Mirage
The Crystal and the Dew
Silver Fountains
Goodbye to Yesterday
In the Melting Pot
Unborn Tomorrow

FOR CHILDREN

Minty
Five Pairs of Hands
Trouble for the Tabors

Minty and the Missing Picture
Minty and the Secret Room
Top Secret

BARBARA GOOLDEN

The Rags of Time

HEINEMANN : LONDON

William Heinemann Ltd
15 Queen Street, Mayfair, London W1X 8BE

LONDON MELBOURNE TORONTO
JOHANNESBURG AUCKLAND

First published 1978
© Barbara Goolden 1978

SBN 434 30212 0

Printed in Great Britain by
Willmer Brothers Limited, Rock Ferry, Merseyside

'Love, all alike, no reason knowes nor clyme
Nor houres, dayes, months which are the rags of time. . . .
                                                            John Donne

Chapter One

SHE STRETCHED in the comfortable warmth of her bed and watched, flickering against the flowered curtains, the teasing sunlight.

Caroline sat up and wished herself a happy birthday. 'Seventy,' she murmured. 'Nobody, of course, will remember : I rather wish that I had given up counting, myself.' Her face, a little pinker down the side on which she had been lying, was reluctantly amused. She never boasted of her ability to meet rebuff, preferring to let other people bruise themselves against so firm a wall of indifference. She was no fighter in her own defence : her retreat was unobtrusive and complete.

'Caro has a fondness for privacy,' said her brother, who thought it peculiar. He himself enjoyed disagreement, believing it to be evidence of wide-mindedness, always provided that he was left with his obstinacy intact.

'Rowley is much too clever to be sensible,' said Caroline, 'he ought to try more, but he won't. I do think university life is hampering. I always hoped he'd make a name for himself, but he lacks eccentricity. Even his very low collars don't help : in fact he might be anyone, as of course he is, but I wish it didn't show.'

The post arrived as she was leaving the bathroom; she assured herself that she did not expect anything, therefore it was illogical to be disappointed to find only a receipt from the Gas Company.

'After all,' reasoned Caroline, 'everybody who once cared for me is dead. I'm perfectly used to it . . . here's Mrs Bird.'

Her daily help, plump and a little breathless, met her in the hall and held out a bunch of limp daffodils wrapped in a scrap of damp newspaper. 'I brought these for your birthday,' she said. 'I remembered the date on account of its being the same as poor old Dad's, and seeing as we had a few left over after we'd been up to the cemetery yesterday. I thought you might like them.'

'I do indeed, bless you. Thank you very much. They're sweet.'

'Yes, well they could do with a drop of water,' returned Mrs Bird modestly, 'because it's a bit warm in my kitchen overnight on account of the boiler, and one of them's bending a bit, but as I always say it's the thought that counts.' And taking off her coat and scarf, she hung them on the hook inside the kitchen door, and added : 'Did you have a nice post?'

'No. I expect my friends consider I'm too old to have birthdays.'

'That you're not, and you don't look it neither. You don't seem to have changed much all the time I've worked for you. One or two of them might have sent you a card I do think. It's always nice to be remembered. The fact is people don't seem to take the trouble like they used to. What with bingo and the pools, they never give a thought to others, and the money the young ones get nowadays! My grandson does a paper round on his bike before he goes to school of a morning, and earns more than I ever got at his age for a full day's work. Talk about scrubbing! These young ones don't know the meaning of putting their backs into nothing. Mr Bird always says a spell in the Navy 'ud teach them! Well, he should know seeing he had twenty years of it, and

8

been bronical ever since. Leave those daffs in here, and I'll put them in water for you, and then I'll be getting on with your breakfast. Will you have your egg scrambled or poached?'

'I don't mind,' said Caroline vaguely. She took small interest in what she ate, and wandered into her little white sitting-room to turn on the radiator and open the windows. Already the thrushes had heard her and clamoured for the biscuit crumbs she tossed them. The day with its accustomed procession of events had begun. She looked up at a thin blue sky without a cloud, and thought of other years when peace was not what she had sought.

It was odd to have outlived happiness and substituted an uncomplaining resignation. The moments of bliss belonged to a lost self. She did not want them back, the mere thought of them was too exhausting. She could no longer accept the burden she had once carried so gladly, she shied from recollection of both joy and grief.

In the peace of her small country home she looked to her flowers, and the friendly birds, and the few simple people for reassurance. Beyond was noise : there was the clash of invading machinery even in the fields; there was too much volubility, declarations of conflicting opinion, of independence, of contempt. There was an ugliness of rapacity, of impatience, of the destruction of gentleness. She avoided all that.

'You let your friends walk over you,' said her brother Rowland.

'If it amuses them,' said Caroline.

'I think they find you irritating.'

'That's unfortunate.'

'Don't you mind?'

'Not particularly. I never interfere with other people's amusements.'

A*

'I suppose you don't like them sufficiently.'

'That could be the reason.'

'How uncomfortable.' For himself he attached importance at least to a mild popularity among the indulgent young whom he piloted towards the attainment of their degrees at Cambridge. He was not easily discouraged by lack of enthusiasm : he read their essays with boredom and was very occasionally surprised by evidence of interest. Bit by bit he became a slightly comical institution, the eventual destiny of many dons. He was known to travel abroad during the Long Vacation, and suspected of enjoying slightly raffish company. In his youth he had been bookish, intelligent, and undisciplined. But what should have been a phase became a rôle. For a middle-aged man to be merely scholarly and a little strange, did not seem very sensible; it limited his resources. He became liked by elderly well-to-do women who made a habit of hospitality in university circles, in the belief that they were entertaining culture. It was even thought at one time that he was a coming man, but he never came, not, to all intents and purposes, ever having started. He was not the kind of economist who might have been useful to eminent politicians, he never sought to write brilliant speeches sprinkled with classical allusions which others less well-endowed might have used with profit; he was much too indolent.

'I suppose, if he had considered it at all, he would have thought it rather pointless to ring me up on my birthday,' decided Caroline. 'After all, he hasn't done it for a long time, and once one drops that kind of thing, it's difficult to start again. I'm sure he thinks he's done as much as can be expected from him when he sends me a pot of flowers for Christmas. And I know I oughtn't to be disappointed if he doesn't make some sort of acknowledgement of the book token I send him. It's childish to mind : it's just a pity that there isn't anyone else.'

She ate her breakfast with the morning paper propped against the coffee pot. The journalists had collected the usual number of disastrous happenings and sordid events. It did not look, reflected Caroline, as if the world was becoming a better place to live in. Yet she was inclined to regard its decay with equanimity. Wars, inhumanity, base desires, consuming self-interest prevailed and she could not feel angry about it any more. The malicious strength of evil received a sufficiency of applause, but she never failed to take refuge in contemplation of the greater power of good. It seemed to her that to trust to a minority of such magnitude brought paradox into relation with truth. Which, after all, said Caroline, was all that mattered.

At no time had she ever asked her brother Rowland what he thought about the riddle of life because he would promptly have become testy. He had, she felt sure, a nervous working arrangement with God which enabled him to stifle any uncomfortable reflections. He could not lay to his own charge anything much worse than a liking for lewd literature; an occasional visit to a fashionable night club abroad, where his slow excellent French was really rather a waste of time; and a cultivated fondness for the enrichment of expensive brandy.

On a totting-up process he could not find anything with which to reproach himself. He kept his temper with all his pupils, having a reluctance to match his irritability against their casual insolence. They were no worse than other young men but he could not command their respect, and therefore he would not risk being made to look a fool.

On the whole he managed very well. Since the tender emotions alarmed him, he was careful to engage in nothing involving his better nature—always assuming that he had one. And of course he had : his sister admitted that. He could be amusing if it suited him, affable in appreciative company, and charming to his elderly and affluent lady friends. To others, whose youth and powers of attraction satisfied him, he behaved with a generosity commensurate with obtaining value for money, and was seldom disappointed.

'I suppose he's happy,' reflected Caroline. 'He has of course never been ambitious. Perhaps it's better he should be like that in order to avoid disillusionment. I suppose he's never had enough courage to take risks.' In the cloistered situation of college life he had not known war. His defective sight and his disinclination had kept him in safe places.

'It wasn't really his fault,' said Caroline.

Here she paused, standing at the window to watch frost's unkind grip release its hold on the bent blades of grass. Sometimes she looked at the ageing men in the fields slowly ploughing the hard earth, and listened to their dragging speech, wondering again at the baffled obedience which had once driven them across the cruel seas towards an alien and bloodstained land. She wondered what they thought about now as they trudged on their tired way home. Machines had taken the place of horses, everything resisted the past; the tied cottages contained bathrooms indifferently appreciated, television sets occupied pride of place in congested sitting-rooms, and oil-fired heaters replaced the friendliness of burning coals. The farm workers, not conspicuously well-rewarded for their labours, looked in the face of what they were assured was progress and were resigned. They had no particular wish to move with the times, the passage was too swift for them. They left it, they said, to the young 'uns.

For her part Caroline missed the children who grew up on the farms and learned the facts of rude life in clean simplicity. But the towns drew them away, there was more money and more distraction in the polluted air of the streets.

'One day,' she decided, 'they'll feel as I do. They'll value peace.'

'Don't you move,' counselled Mrs Bird, when she came in with a tin of polish and several leathers. 'I'll just do over your floor after I've given your rugs a shake outside. I don't know where all the dust comes from, I'm sure. I reckon it's because of you being so set on open windows. I wonder you don't catch cold more often.' And subsiding on her fat knees, she added : 'There's one thing I will say for parquet, it does pay for keeping nice . . . There's someone at the door and look at m' hands !'

'I'll go,' said Caroline in her leisurely fashion. She never hurried; haste was for the young to whom time was so important; they had so much of it that they spent it with careless freedom. It was restful, she found, to lose the desire for rapidity.

Sunshine had strayed across the little hall over the worn oak chest, dented and scarred, and the shallow copper bowl which had once held a shower of visiting cards.

'Thank goodness,' said Caroline, 'no one drops them on me any more.'

She opened the front door, and suddenly laughed with delight because her visitor was so very small and so pretty.

'Why, Rosie,' she said, 'how lovely to see you !'

'Yes,' said her caller placidly, and looked up with very clear blue eyes. She held out a large envelope fastened with a red seal and addressed in big unsteady letters.

'It's for you,' explained Rosie, 'because it's your birthday.'

Caroline planted a gentle kiss on the fair silky head. 'Thank you, sweetheart, how perfectly lovely.'

'There's a picture inside, I did it for you.' Watching intently to see nothing was missed, she went on : 'That's the sea, and that's a boat, and that's me and Mummy and Daddy bathing, and that's Daddy's moustache but I had to do it green because I hadn't got any more brown. Do you like it?'

'I think it's *beautiful*. Is that a fish in the corner?'

'No, it's my baby brother; he hasn't come yet because he's still in Mummy's tummy, but he'll come soon. P'raps tomorrow. Are you going to have a party for your birthday? I had a pink cake with four candles an' I blew them all out by myself. Jane wanted to, but her Mummy didn't let her.'

'Now, who is Jane?'

'My best friend, but I hate her. She broke my balloon.'

'I expect it was an accident.'

'No, it wasn't ... She's *hollible* ... I've got to go now. Mummy's waiting for me ... Goodbye.'

'Goodbye, poppet, and thank you for the lovely card.' She watched the small flying figure run through the open garden gate towards a young woman in a trouser suit, standing by a large, rather battered car.

'Happy birthday, Caroline,' she called in a sugary treble. 'Have fun.' And drove away at speed.

'The way they go on!' observed Mrs Bird at the sitting-room door. 'Mind you don't slip now, go careful. I've come down meself more than the once in m' own place after I been polishing. Fancy her calling you by your first name, and young enough to be your grand-daughter! "*Have fun*" indeed! What does she expect, I'd like to know?'

'I thought it sounded rather nice,' said Caroline. 'Anyhow it was kindly meant. Look at Rosie's card.'

Mrs Bird chuckled. 'She's done her father's moustache all right, hasn't she? They was all on the beach when me and Mr Bird passed by that hot Sunday we had, and he remarked to me he didn't think it was decent, not in her condition, and no attempt to cover it up. Well, I'd better stop talking else I'll never get the floor finished and make a start on your curtains.'

Caroline propped her birthday card against the empty crystal vase on the mantelpiece. She felt again the child's soft hair beneath her palms and the smoothness of the white forehead where she had kissed it. She liked the casual inconsequence of children, their butterfly lingering, their swift airy departure. A little of their company nowadays suited her very well. It was not restfulness that she sought from them but the opportunity to live for a little while on their level. There she could find simplicity and be untroubled by the world of stress.

But as she returned to her chair, she felt unexpectedly saddened. After all, this day was just like any other day. Tomorrow she would not have the absurdity of a denied anticipation; there was nothing large left. Triviality dwelt in all her happenings : little was stressed except caution. *Be careful not to slip on the stairs, watch the traffic when you cross the road, don't strain your eyes, don't go out when it's foggy . . .*

It was not in all probability as though people genuinely cared what became of her, they merely said the expected thing. She knew that they would think it in very poor taste if she told them she was really not in the least interested in self-preservation. It seemed pointless to exercise care merely for the sake of continuing a colourless existence. But like so much else in life, it was a discipline to be accepted without reference to personal preference.

'Why don't you go to the pictures this afternoon?' asked Mrs Bird, returning to thrust the daffodils with much firmness into the crystal vase. 'It would make a change for you, on your birthday and all.'

'You know I never go to the cinema,' protested Caroline, to whom the distractions of a small country town made no appeal at all. 'If I felt like wasting petrol—which I don't— I'd go and get my hair done. But I can't bother.'

'Well, I will say it looks all right to me being it curls natural. Was you thinking of having one or two of your friends in to tea this afternoon?'

'I was not. I enjoy my own company, you know.'

'If you was to ask me, I'd say you had too much of it. It don't do anyone good to get into a rut.'

'I love my rut,' declared Caroline obstinately. She supposed that it was true. She had long learned that distraction merely pushed distress—if any existed—aside, to return later undiminished. Quiet was more likely to encourage a better sense of proportion. To be alone was not a hardship, but the incessant battle of gossiping women wearied her. In her opinion it was seldom charitable. But she felt unaccountably depressed as the day travelled slowly on. She was glad to see Mrs Bird depart, yet when she settled by the fire and took up her book, it failed to capture her attention. The picture it drew of contemporary social life bored her. Admittedly some people's experiences were more shapely than her own, but she looked in vain for an acknowledgement of life's strange paradoxes and of the delight of unexpected happenings.

'It makes me feel as if they never walked towards anything but a cul-de-sac ... Good heavens, what on earth's that?' She opened the window to look out and saw a small car on the grass with her little fence festooned round its bonnet. A very young man stepped over the tangled wire and came towards her in abject apology.

'Oh,' he said, 'I'm most terribly sorry. Your lane's a bit slippery after the rain, and I'm afraid I skidded. Of course, I'll pay for the damage.'

'I'll come out and have a look at it,' said Caroline. She closed the window and took a coat from the hall chest. She felt rather sorry for the boy, he looked so upset.

'It's not the first time this has happened,' she said, as she

16

joined him. 'I really ought to put up a new fence. You've cut your hand quite badly, haven't you? You'd better come indoors and wash it.'

'It's frightfully kind of you : it's nothing very much.'

'Only dirty wire and jagged at that! Come along. I keep a first-aid kit in my kitchen.'

He nodded, his lips compressed, his pale face twitching with the effort to maintain composure.

Caroline, with a touch on his elbow, guided him into the kitchen and sat him down beside the sink. 'You'd better have some brandy,' she said, 'you'll be all right in a minute . . . put your head between your knees.'

He was as docile as a child, and when he stretched a cold hand to take his drink, grinned sheepishly. 'I'm awfully sorry,' he said again, 'it's nothing, I've got a very slightly dickey heart and it plays up a bit now and then.'

She nodded and poured antiseptic into a small bowl, adding warm water. 'Let me have a look at your hand . . . that's all right . . . You won't need stitching : silly sort of thing to do, wasn't it? How long have you had your car?'

'About a week . . . I had two shots at the test before I passed.' He winced and screwed his eyes up while she took a wad of cotton wool and gently washed the blood away.

'Good boy . . . it's bound to sting a bit.'

'I had a tetanus injection last term at school when I gashed my knee playing football. I won't have to have another, will I?'

'No, don't worry. Are you fond of football?'

'No . . . I'm not much good.'

'Do you like cricket better?'

'Well actually, I'm not much use at that either.' He sipped the brandy and added : 'It annoys my father frightfully. He's terribly disappointed that I'm pretty hopeless at games. He was a tremendous success himself. I don't think he likes people of my age much. He married rather late actually : too late, I expect.'

'Are you an only son?'

'Yes. If I'd had a brother it wouldn't have mattered so much . . . Ow! I'm sorry, that's a bit sore.'

'Never mind, I've almost finished. Tell your mother I suggest you leave the bandages on until tomorrow and then perhaps show your doctor.'

He looked embarrassed. 'I shan't be seeing her until next week. She and my father are divorced. I live with her and my stepfather most of the time . . . she's awfully sweet. She didn't really want me to have a car but my father gave it to me for a birthday present.'

'Are you interested in cars?'

'No, not really. He thinks I ought to be.'

'When do you leave school?'

'At the end of next term, thank goodness.'

'Don't you like it?'

'Well—in a way, I suppose.'

'What do you want to do?'

'I'm not sure really.' His smooth face with its greenish pallor became a little sulky.

'I expect everybody asks you that,' she said sympathetically. 'I'm sorry, I ought to have remembered.'

He watched her long fingers unrolling a bandage. 'Most people don't understand : you obviously do. I suppose you've got sons?'

'No, I'm not married.'

'Oh . . . I'm sorry . . . I mean, you look as though you were.'

'What a nice thing to say.'

'Why? Do you think it's nicer to be married?'

'In some ways, most ways probably. Keep your wrist still . . . Does that feel too tight?'

'No, it's all right.' He yawned and closed his eyes.

'Finish your brandy.' She steadied his wrist. 'And when you're ready come into the next room and lie on my sofa for half an hour.'

'Can I really? I'm frightfully sorry to be a nuisance . . . How much do you think it will cost to mend your fence?'

'Next to nothing. My gardener-cum-handyman will see to it in the morning.'

'Oh! I mean . . . this is awful . . . couldn't I . . .?'

'No, you couldn't,' said Caroline, 'don't be silly. My gardener's an old age pensioner and there's very little to do in a small place like mine at this time of year, so he'll be quite pleased to have something to occupy him. Do you live in the country?'

'When I'm with my mother. My stepfather used to breed polo ponies.'

'That's rather fun : do you like horses?'

'Not very much. I used to get asthma. I don't often now, but riding used to bring it on. I was allergic to horse hair or something. I must say my stepfather's very nice about it.'

'You get on with him?'

'Yes, I do, up to a point. He's rather by way of being constantly facetious : he makes jokes all the time and laughs loudly at everything. But he's very amiable.'

'Come along into the next room. What's your name by the way?'

'Sandy Orme . . . Oh, shall I empty that water for you? Some of it's gone over the table a bit.'

'No,' she said a little sharply. 'I'll see to it presently.'

He followed her into the living-room, looking snubbed. He nursed his bandaged hand tenderly to remind her to treat him with consideration.

'Sit down,' she said, 'I'm going to take your shoes off . . . Don't be silly, you can't manage by yourself, and I'd rather not have muddy marks on my sofa.'

'Sorry,' he said unhappily.

From her knees she looked at him more intently, but whether in relief or disappointment she hardly knew. 'I used to know someone of your name years ago. Alexander Orme : he was in the Gunners.'

The boy grinned rather wanly. 'That's my father. Actually he's retired of course. He had a smashing time during the War.'

'Did anyone? However, I suppose it's possible. He was a fine soldier,' said Caroline.

'Oh, did you like him? How funny ... well perhaps it isn't. Women usually do : I can never think why. He's frightfully dictatorial.'

'Perhaps that is why. Come and lie down now. You'd better have this rug over your knees. Are you feeling warmer?'

'Yes thanks. I'm awfully sorry to be such a nuisance ... I don't even know your name ...'

'Caroline Chandler.'

'I must tell my father when I get back. He's got a fantastic number of friends. When they start boring him, he drops them.'

'He didn't have the chance with me.'

Young Sandy climbed on to the sofa. 'What did you say?'

'Nothing. I'm going to draw the curtains and leave you to yourself for a while.'

'Where will you be?'

'In my kitchen. Shut your eyes and go to sleep.'

'All right.' He snuggled down and pulled a fold of the blanket over his head.

'What an extraordinary coincidence,' she told herself, as she went away to pour the stained water down the sink and replace the little bottle of antiseptic in its box. 'Anyhow,

I hope the boy won't tell Alex : nothing would exasperate him more than to be reminded of me.'

She had long overcome the acuteness of memory. The whole thing was deeply buried beneath the layers of merciful time. To outlive pain was the final triumph.

But as she washed her hands under the kitchen tap and dried them on the rough roller towel, she forgot familiar things and, with a sudden sharp stab of recollection, recalled what she had done. Useless to cling to pride and cherish untruth, if so simple a happening as a boy's appearance could destroy her peace and make nonsense of the work of years.

Chapter Two

'So SWEET of you to be kind to my boy,' said Mrs Garland, her head aslant and her expression silly. 'I never wanted him to have a car but Alex paid no attention. Sandy might have been killed!'

'Nearly never killed a man,' said Tom Garland, and chuckled happily. He was a short, rubicund person whose perpetual amiability expressed itself in loud and cheerful noises. Milly, his wife, finding him a refreshing contrast to her first husband, was devoted to him.

'I hoped,' Caroline told them, 'you wouldn't mind my letting the garage people take Sandy's car away for a complete overhaul, but I know they're really reliable, and it's as well to make assurance doubly sure.'

Milly gazed at her with respect. She thought that people who made that sort of comment—which sounded *almost* like a quotation—must be very clever.

Sandy, looking pale and worried, sat in his mother's garden room, nervously warming his hands against the hot water pipes. 'Father will be frightfully annoyed at my coming here instead of going back to London,' he said.

'Let him blow his top,' interrupted Tom, 'don't worry. You were in luck's way finding someone who is nice enough to take having a smashed fence as all in the day's work. To say nothing of doing a very efficient piece of first-aid work on your hand.'

'Poor *darling*,' said Milly, gazing at her son with a regretful sentimentality. 'I've not had a happy moment since you passed your test.'

'That for a tale!' commented Tom, and patted her knee affectionately. 'My dear wife,' he assured Caroline, 'underestimates her own powers of endurance to an astounding degree. When I go down for the day to Bosham to sail my little boat, she has a rapturous time at home, playing bridge for the whole afternoon and evening, winning infinitesimal sums from her long-suffering friends, and then rushing into the hall on my return to fling herself on my manly bosom in floods of tears, having, of course, assumed I'd been lost overboard.'

'Tom, you *are* naughty!' bleated his gratified wife. 'How can you say such things? And you know perfectly well I never play for more than a shilling a hundred because I think gambling's wrong. Don't you?'

'No,' said Caroline.

Tom grinned. 'Good for you.'

'I never feel a sweepstake is *quite* the same,' Milly Garland told them. 'Especially when it's for a good cause.'

'Didn't you once win a bottle of bubbly on a sixpenny ticket at a church fête?' said Sandy suddenly, and immediately became hot with confusion.

'I remember Alex made me give it away to the curate,' said his mother, 'because he said it was bound to be undrinkable, but that the poor man wouldn't know any better. I'm afraid it wasn't very kind.'

'That wouldn't have worried Alex,' said her husband, looking a little uncomfortable.

Caroline watched the trio without smiling: if she was aware that her silence was unco-operative, it did not appear to disturb her.

Milly said: 'We can't all think alike.' Her round blue

23

eyes looked at Tom for reassurance, her plump little hands smoothed the silk skirt strained across her thighs.

The boy, watching her, seemed embarrassed as if her capacity for foolish comment made him feel insecure. And yet he loved her because she was gentle : he liked her fluffy grey hair and her full pink cheeks. Sometimes, when they were alone, she cradled his head against her bosom and he enjoyed the scent of carnations.

'Tom is going to take us to see that play at the Adelphi next week,' she said. 'That'll be fun, won't it, Sandy?'

'Yes, terrific,' he said. He knew he was expected to be enthusiastic. He wanted to go, but it reminded him of the approaching end of the holidays.

'Lots of lovely girls kicking their legs about with heavenly abandon, I shall have to be chained to my stall,' said Tom.

'Don't be naughty, darling,' repeated his wife once again, watching him with fond approval.

Sandy sighed and achieved a weak smile. He glanced at Caroline, who got up.

'I must go,' she said. 'I'll tell my garage to contact you direct. I know them sufficiently well to feel morally certain they won't release the car unless they're satisfied that everything's in order.'

'I really can't thank you enough,' said Milly, 'we're all so very grateful to you, aren't we, Sandy?' Her small high voice encouraged him to say the right thing : he wished she wouldn't : it was no good her trying to make him a social success : she was never cross because of her failure, she just went on trying.

'Odd though it may seem we'd rather have him intact,' said Tom, 'if for no better reason than I need his help with the manure load which, while slightly nifty already, will be delightfully rich next week. Useful chap our Sandy.'

Caroline, listening to the prolonged merriment of husband

and wife, in which they were joined by the reluctant boy, was glad to get away. It seemed surprising that Alex should have married such a goose, but even stranger that Milly had had the gumption to run away from him.

But as she drove she grew kinder; she could well imagine that so patently tender-hearted and foolish a woman would have had to seek sanctuary from Alex when opportunity offered. It was only astonishing that it had not happened sooner. There had been, it was said, arguments and tears, there were endless scenes and, finally, there was an occasion when he gripped his wife's shoulders and flung her spinning against the wall. Milly fled to the welcoming arms of Tom Garland, and an enraged Alex immediately instituted divorce proceedings.

Those who admired Alex Orme said he had been disgracefully treated : he was not grateful for their sympathy, resenting deeply his humiliation. There were unfortunately no convenient wars to which he might have transferred himself, seeking glory. He served in Ireland as the next best thing, and held a staff job in Berlin, and at the War Office he made himself respected, if not universally liked.

Since his ex-wife had been granted the custody of their infant son with suitable access to himself, he did not, owing to Sandy's extreme youth and delicacy, avail himself of his dubious privilege, and not until the boy's adolescence did he take the least interest in him. Their relationship from the start was uneasy. Alex was aware that Tom Garland—whom he considered a fool—was more successful in gaining the boy's confidence than he was. He claimed pressure of military duty as an excuse for avoiding seeing his son more than once or twice a year.

However Alex had always needed Caroline's admiration because, as everybody knew, success was meat and drink to him. His only failure had been his marriage and he could not blame himself for that. It had been all Milly's fault because she was stupid and immature : and Tom Garland, being a fool, had swallowed her hard luck story, hook, line and sinker.

All this he had expected Caroline to accept without question. Being the woman she was, and possessing a wholesome measure of scepticism, she had believed as much as she thought necessary. The mistake she made was to fall in love with Alex. It was not altogether surprising. He had good looks, intelligence and a great deal of spasmodic charm. When he was assured of congenial company, he could be delightful. His contemporaries admired him for an outstanding sportsman, for a discreet womanizer, and one who was not only determined on the main chance but invariably successful in obtaining it. He was renowned for the shortness of his temper, his ability to forget his own offences, and his capacity to drink more than the majority of his fellows with considerably less ill effect. No one had ever seen Alex drunk or even fuddled. Whatever he may have been like in private, in public he maintained good manners—always assuming that a degree of bad temper was not considered damaging to the whole concept of the man.

He had met Caroline when he was on leave from Berlin : he was not certain that he altogether liked her but he found her very attractive and he was determined to make her like him. This proved more difficult than he expected. He had not before met a woman who resisted him at his best and he could not think why she did it. He was never subtle and it would not have seemed possible to him that she should be attracted and yet so loth to admit it.

Caroline herself had no such difficulty in analysing her situation. She considered it extremely disturbing. There were occasions when she found Alex trivial, thick-skinned and bombastic. All that she disliked very much. But she admired

26

physical courage, self-confidence, and most of the qualities which went to the creating of a good soldier. He had, as well, an entirely masculine make-up, and she who was intolerant of much that she observed in the female character, valued the dominance which he exercised. She made some attempt to avoid it without realizing that she was doing the very thing which excited him to further effort. She knew that she annoyed him but she could not help herself. Possibly she did not want to.

But she found him progressively upsetting. Her brother, Rowley, with whom she shared a flat in Cambridge, was not the sort of person whose advice she cared to ask. She knew very well that the indulgence he found necessary to permit himself, did not extend to his sister. In accordance with many men of his sort, he expected a high standard of morality among the female members of his family : it seemed right and proper, and to some extent encouraged that sheepish sensation of apology which invariably accompanied any lapses from grace on his own part.

Caroline rather despised him. She found nothing of the same sort to despise in Alex who, it was apparent, never suffered from conscientious scruples where his own satisfaction was concerned. She had not before met a man who so unblushingly made no concession to other people's feelings. In her own family—with the exception of her brother, the men had been clerical schoolmasters of unblemished reputation whose recreations were chess, fishing, and indifferent health.

Caroline's father, having married very late, fathered a couple of children and died, presumably from surprise, shortly afterwards, to be followed a year or two later by his aggrieved widow, who considered that he had no business to abandon her.

The children were brought up by grandparents, with an

innocent belief in boarding schools and the society of their contemporaries. The indolent Rowley discovered a life spent in the enervating climate of Cambridge and the society of casual young men, suited him very well, the vacations supplying him with sufficient contrast to so much required decorum. Caroline, deprived in infancy of loving parents, became attached to her nurse and her teddy bear. Finding neither responsive, she endured school with rather more youthful detachment than most children. She was quicker than her brother and less well-educated.

At the age of nineteen she was seduced by a delightful young man in the Air Force and found the performance disappointing. No ill-effects resulting, she told herself she would not do it again unless she fell in love. The Flight Lieutenant did his best to persuade her that this was in fact what had happened, but she continued to disagree with him, and was no more than ordinarily sorry when the young man, whose high spirits were not quenched by her repeated refusals, played high jinks in the air and crashed.

'He loved showing off, bless him,' said Caroline.

Feeling that it was incumbent upon her to earn her own living and not rely upon a very small private income, she obtained a job as secretary to the head of a well-established firm of provincial solicitors. There she worked for ten years without appreciable boredom until Alex Orme walked into her life. There was nothing significant in their first meeting; he arrived too early for his appointment with the senior partner, and was furnished with a back number of *Country Life* and an ash tray. Caroline at her desk continued to type. Alex continued to read an article on Gun Dogs. After some ten minutes a buzzer at Caroline's side emitted a brief hoarse noise.

She got up and glanced at her companion. 'Mr Frewin will see you now,' she said.

Alex, following her, paused at the door and afforded her a sufficiently comprehensive glance. He said nothing and Caroline paid no attention as she led the way towards the office marked 'Private'.

Back at her own desk she spent the next half hour finding concentration on her work a little difficult.

'And what,' later on, said Mr Frewin, the senior partner, a rotund easy-going man with a pink bald head, 'what did you think of Captain Orme?'

'Do I have to think anything?'

'From what I hear most women do.'

'Hurray for them,' said Caroline flatly.

The old man looked amused. 'Would you like to know what he said about you when he came in here?'

'Not particularly.'

'I'm sure he meant me to tell you.'

'Well he won't know that you haven't, will he?'

'I've no doubt he'll ask me. He's coming again today week.'

'Why?'

'Your guess is as good as mine. I've a shrewd suspicion you're the attraction.'

Caroline sighed with impatience. 'Mr Frewin, I don't really think that's very funny.'

His smile was indulgent. 'It wasn't meant to be. Anyhow, my dear, you keep him at arm's length. I don't think I should trust him further than I can see him. No doubt he has the highest principles where his career is concerned. That sort often have.'

'What sort, Mr Frewin?'

'Fellows with a low standard of sexual morality, my dear, on the quiet, of course.'

'That's all very satisfactory for him then.'

'One supposes so. He's got means and I've an idea he spends it.'

'Why not. Isn't that what money's for?'

She had not been interested in Alex's private affairs, nor did she appreciate old Mr Frewin's veiled hints against him. All the same she was aware of being annoyed when an appointment was made for Captain Orme, a little pointedly, in her absence.

'He asked after you,' said the old man, his kindly smile creasing his fat, benevolent face. 'He asked me where my very attractive secretary had got to. I explained that you were in the local courts, for the purpose of taking shorthand notes concerning a case in which counsel we employed had a watching brief. Whereupon . . .' Mr Frewin checked himself, 'you're not listening, Miss Chandler.'

'Yes, I am.'

'I beg your pardon. Anyhow, Captain Orme was good enough to remark that in his opinion the county court was an unbecoming background . . . I am only quoting him, my dear . . . for a seductive young woman.'

'To which you replied?'

'I changed the subject.'

'So I should hope. Who on earth does he think he is?' . . .

It was odd how she remembered their conversation over the long bridge of years. She recalled that she was not altogether pleased to come across him a couple of weeks later on the towpath of the river, watching sweating young men rowing with set expressions of painful determination.

'Do you often take time off from the office?' he asked.

'No,' said Caroline.

He stood in front of her. 'I've finished such business as I had with old Frewin, which occurs to me as being a pity.'

She looked inattentive, watching the boat.

'Will you lunch with me on Sunday? At the University Arms, at one?'

'No, I don't think so,' said Caroline, 'thank you.'

'That's odd because I *do* think so. I should enjoy it. I'll drive over to fetch you. You might even introduce me to your brother. Come along, don't play about with me.'

'I'm not in the habit of "playing about" with anyone.'

'No, I didn't think you were. That's settled then, isn't it?'

She had laughed a little and capitulated. She had forgotten that it was rather fun to be told what to do. At once he had become much more companionable. He tried most of the usual gambits with her and failed. He drove her across the flat Cambridgeshire country in his car, he was impatient, and rather angry, and surprisingly placating.

'I can't make you out,' he said, 'how old are you?'

'I'm thirty : why?'

'You look much less.'

She remembered very clearly the varied tones of his very agreeable voice and failed to care that they were practised. She kept him in check when his kisses disturbed her, his fondling made her restless.

'Why not?' he had complained when she put him away. 'Why not?'

Very soon he insisted that he loved her; it was more of a protest than a declaration. He sent her flowers, he demanded every spare moment of her time, he even lost something of his arrogance. 'I'm damned if I know what you want,' he said, 'it isn't marriage and children, you told me that yourself. Then what?'

If she had said a different quality of love, he would in all probability have told her she was looking for something which didn't exist. He was simple and lustful and genuinely perplexed.

'I'm sick of all this,' he complained. 'It's hell, I'm even

31

sick of the Army and the whole dam' show. You've made a
mess of everything for me.'

'That's not fair. You started it all. It hasn't been exactly
peaceful for me, has it?'

'Why not? . . . no, look at me, Caroline, tell me the truth.'

'I have told you the truth.'

'Never . . . never at any time. Your whole idea is to keep
out of my reach. When I hold you in my arms you're not
really there . . . I don't know how the devil to manage you.
And the incredible thing is you love me, don't you? Don't
you, Caroline?'

It was difficult to remember exactly how much she had
admitted. Or how little. The natural ardour of her whole
nature was restrained by a conviction that no truth existed
between them. The brief experimental encounter with the
young Flight-Lieutenant was no parallel. No deep feeling
had been involved with him, and little cheapness. It left
no bitterness behind it, and only a mild degree of disappointment. To Caroline it was merely something which had
happened and could be thrust into the background of her
mind, not entirely forgotten because of the state of disillusionment, but no more than that.

With Alex, because her whole heart was involved, she was
determined to keep her head. She had no plan, she was not
happy, but she felt within reach of ecstasy. She did not want
it; she wished he had not come her way. She did not wish
to be interrupted. But she had a sense of a new beginning
although she had no idea what she meant by that.

'*How old are you, Caroline?*'

'*I'm thirty.*'

'*You look much less*' . . .

Sitting alone in her room she did not want to unroll the
past and flinch from the futility of it all. It was all such a
long time ago. She wished that the boy had not ditched

his cheap little car outside her home. There was nothing in him to remind her of Alex except his long bones and his smooth pallor, but it was not resemblance which caused her pain now. It was a re-entry of irresistible memory, of something which had had greater power to crucify her spirit than any act of physical violation. She had held on to her pride though it meant the death of her love. She knew even in old age that she would not have had it otherwise. She could not be so utterly untrue to her belief in a standard of conduct as to stand by as a spectator of savage cruelty.

It had happened at the end of a polo match when the well-dressed crowd was slowly moving away, and the military band were lined up to march off. A couple of frisking fox terriers had invaded the emptying ground to chase each other with an enthusiasm which had caused Caroline's spaniel to slip his lead and join in the fun.

Alex's young pony startled by the noisy scuffle, reared up and bolted. The dogs scattered, and Alex caught unawares was thrown. Sickened, she had watched him scramble to his feet, his face darkened in fury as he reversed his stick and struck the pony savagely across its head. The circling spaniel fled, to return bewildered, and cannoned against the heavy foot lifted to swing against its side.

'Stop that, you brute ...' She heard her own horrified voice join with the little dog's shrill scream.

The thinning crowd paused to see what was going on. Someone came over to take the trembling pony's rein and lead him away, and Caroline had the yelping spaniel gathered in her arms. A young player, taking off his cap to show a hot worried face, spoke to her, saying she hardly knew what. She supposed she answered mechanically, hurrying across the ground at his side towards the gates and a small waiting car.

'Better make sure he's okay, spaniels are frightfully sensi-

33

B

tive,' said the young man, as he climbed in beside her. 'Hullo, he's licking your fingers : I don't think he's much hurt. There's a good vet at this end of the town : what the devil made that fool kick the poor little chap ? It wasn't one of our side, thank God . . . You feeling all right?'

She nodded, and whispered to the small quivering spaniel whose whimpers were subsiding. She remembered later that the vet had a beard and very gentle hands. 'Couple of broken ribs,' he said, 'but he'll do : I'll give him a sedative now and you'd better repeat the dose tonight. Keep him in his basket and as quiet as you can for a few days. Ring me up if you want me.'

The helpful young man drove them home. 'Glad to have been of use. Spaniels are frightfully temperamental. My wife is very keen on them but I like something slightly larger and a bit less sentimental myself. Well, I hope the invalid will soon be fit. The chap who kicked him ought to be pole-axed.'

Sitting in her kitchen with the dog, snug in his blanketed basket at her feet, she had been unable to stop shivering. She had not before experienced the emotion of hate, which was made additionally difficult by being complex. Cruelty she had always loathed, and unbridled anger seemed to her contemptible.

Yet, against all that, she had been deeply disturbed by a personality more compelling than any she had known before. She had found herself captured by it, without any conscious reasoning or explanation on her part. And when she saw another side to it, she had to come to terms, not with his character, but with her own. To her, loyalty was not adjustable. Once convinced of the disruptive power of love, she accepted it, but in secret. She would not bargain with principle : it seemed to her better to endure self-imposed bereavement than to betray her belief in the necessity for restraint and the control of ungovernable impulse.

The sleeping spaniel stirred but was not wakened by the tears which fell upon his silky head . . .

Caroline listened to the little clock on her mantelpiece striking midnight. Her birthday was over, and the unquiet ghosts of memory retreated once again.

Chapter Three

'I QUITE like your father. I mean I think it's wonderful of him to keep it up . . .'

'Keep *what* up?' interrupted Sandy. But he knew and he didn't care to hear. Walking back from the cinema to which Alex had despatched him in the company of a very young and pretty girl, he felt inadequate. Elizabeth, his father had told him, was a liberal education, but he wanted to run away. He was glad that he was returning to the country next day, to the foolishness of his mother, to Tom Garland's perpetual jollity. That at least was familiar. And in October there would be his first term at Cambridge but he was not going to think about that yet.

'Oh, you know what I mean,' the fresh little face beside him looked scornful. 'He's got a marvellous figure for his age, and he dances divinely, but you can't get away from it he *is* an old boy. I'm rather surprised he hasn't dropped his little games, he's been at it a bit too long. An uncle of mine who knew him in the Army says he was quite a wow once.'

'All right. He may have been, so what?'

'Sorry, I didn't know you liked him.'

'I don't particularly.'

The long street seemed endless. He wished that he were walking over the Downs by himself. He wanted to smell grass and clover, and to capture, if only in imagination, the clean breath of the distant sea.

36

'You're awfully young for your age, aren't you?'

He edged away and said : 'In point of fact you don't know how old I am. As it happens I'm eighteen.'

'Well,' she retorted, 'you wouldn't be leaving school next term if you weren't, unless you'd been sacked. Don't you *want* to grow up? You'll be awfully out of things at Cambridge if you hang on to the Peter Pan image.'

'Thanks very much.'

'Are you offended? I'm only saying it for your own good, you know. I'm younger than you are, but I wouldn't mind betting I know a lot more.'

It had always been the same : at his private school other boys had invariably been anxious to provide him with a good deal of inaccurate sexual information; at his public school, friends attended to his further education with a conscientious regard for advanced learning. He wished that they would shut up, but they never did. The subject seemed inexhaustible.

'I'm going to a party tonight,' she was saying. 'I can bring anyone I like. Would you like to come?'

'No thanks. I don't really like parties. It's very nice of you to ask me.'

'You didn't really enjoy that film, did you?' She was teasing him now and he hated it. 'You were shocked, weren't you?'

'No, of course I wasn't : I—I was just bored with all that bedroom stuff.'

'You *are* a drip really. It was marvellous. They turned the lights off much too soon. *And* the sound track, or whatever it's called. I suppose your father thought it was rather a good joke.'

'Joke?'

'Well, I imagine he thinks it's about time you woke up.'

He looked white and said nothing. They walked past the

37

wide blocks of new flats, the freshly dug flower beds with the tight begonia buds, in the paved courtyards, and everything belonged to an age he didn't understand. It was easier to walk in lonely places where there were no people and no emotions. Presently he would read History at Cambridge and be undisturbed by the ghosts of lost follies, of forgotten heresies, while he turned the stained pages of the past and saw the people within them as no more than thoughts in other men's minds.

'Well, bye-bye,' said the off-hand little voice beside him. 'Here's where I live, plus doting parents and dotty sister.'

'Is she really bonkers?'

'As good as. She's been hauled up twice for driving her car when she was tight, and once for smoking cannabis. She was engaged to a chap who started her on that. He's inside now. She says she's going to marry him when he comes out. She *is* a fool because she's frightfully pretty, and he's a mess.'

'Can't your father stop it?'

' 'Course not, she's over age. I'd like to see poor old Daddy trying to stop either of us doing anything we really wanted to. He used to be in the Navy, but he can't manage us to save his life, poor chap. Well, I must dash. See you again some time. Bye-bye.'

'Bye-bye,' said Sandy mechanically. He thought it a childish sort of farewell. Anyhow, *that* was over.

A few minutes' walk brought him to another block, almost indistinguishable from the one he had just left. He wondered why people liked living in places whose expensive outward appearance was deliberately uniform. Even the poorer cottages in the country, to which he was accustomed, seemed to have more individuality : they were homes in which people accepted all that happened to them with a grumbling philosophy. They did not suppose that they would easily escape from life's harsh discipline, nor did they think very much of those who kicked against the pricks. Their resentment, when they admitted it, was directed against nature because of ruined crops in times of flood or drought. Nature was their friend or their enemy. In their small community they shared disaster or satisfaction in a mutual mood without excitement. They took what came, living close to the earth which nurtured or buried them.

Young Sandy wished that he could achieve their detachment and the rough dignity which men of the soil seemed to him to possess. By the time that he reached his father's flat his self-distrust had increased. He was sure that he would say the wrong thing : he had a headache and the central heating in Alex's study made the air seem dry.

'Well, did you enjoy yourself?' The thin man sitting with long crossed legs in an easy chair, turned his neat head and went on : 'I shrewdly suspect Elizabeth did.'

'Oh—Oh, yes, she—she thought it wonderful.'

'And you didn't?' The scored lines in Alex's face deepened in a slightly malicious smile. 'She would, of course. Pretty little monkey, isn't she?'

'Yes.' He sat down and looked nervously at his father. The gift of speech seemed denied him.

'They dine here at the barbarous hour of half-past seven,' Alex told him. 'In the ordinary way I'm never in. You'd better wash your hands before we go down and get some of that filthy stuff off your knuckles.'

'It's stuck, I think. It's from the plaster that kept my bandage in place. Mother said it would wear off in time.'

'I was under the impression that was Caroline's repair work.'

'Who? Oh—oh, yes, it was. But Mother said it had better have another dressing on in a day or two. It's practically all right now.'

'Then clean up the surrounding mess with a nail brush

and turpentine : there's some in the bathroom.'

'Yes. Now?'

'I said before dinner.'

'Oh, sorry. Yes, of course.'

Alex lit a cigar. 'What,' he asked, 'does Caroline look like now?'

'Well, she—she's rather old, isn't she? She—she looks patient.'

'That's an odd sort of comment. What d'you mean, weary?'

The boy wrinkled his forehead in an effort to explain himself. 'Not exactly that. She's rather pale and her hair's sort of silvery-grey, and she's awfully thin.'

'That's not exactly becoming. Incidentally, I imagine that loss of weight is not something that afflicts your mother. Milly was never exactly a sylph.'

Sandy flushed. 'She looks sweet,' he said, and his voice was unsteady.

'I'm sure she'd be delighted to hear you say so. What are you looking so vexed about?'

'Nothing.'

'Tom's still in the land of the living, I suppose?'

'Yes. *Of course.*'

'Well you needn't sound so annoyed, I only asked a perfectly simple question. Would you like a drink?'

'No thanks.'

'I forgot, you don't drink, do you? When I was your age . . . Oh well, never mind. Please yourself. You're more your mother's responsibility than mine, or if not, that apparently is the way you want it.' He got up to unlock the cellaret. 'Brandy,' he said, 'was my father's downfall, he might have made his name at the Bar if he hadn't preferred otherwise. I've got a better head than he ever had, apart from which, I've never seen the point of confining myself to one voice.' Bringing his drink back to his chair, he sat down and glanced at Sandy's embarrassed face. 'I'm rather thinking of living abroad,' he said. 'Paris, in my opinion, is the most civilized city in the world. That woman, Caroline, hated the French, or if she didn't hate them, she lumped them all together and said they were immoral . . . No, I've got it wrong, that wasn't Caroline, it was your mother. Not that she was any great shakes herself . . .'

'It wasn't her fault,' said Sandy indignantly, 'you drove her to it . . . you were frightfully unkind . . .'

'She told you that, did she?'

'No, Tom did.'

Alex's face grew hot as he expressed with considerable freedom his uncomplimentary opinion of Milly's husband.

'I—I don't know why you say that,' returned Sandy, 'I like him and—and so do most people.'

'That's as it may be,' retorted Alex, 'and you can keep your blasted opinion to yourself.'

'All right, but it's a true one.' He felt frightened, but if he was startled by his own unexpected championship, he was determined to maintain it.

'The trouble with you,' said his father, 'is that none of your opinions are your own. You haven't got the guts to make up your mind for yourself. And, quite obviously, you believe what you're told, which makes you look a fool. I've no doubt Elizabeth tried on her usual game of boasting about her sister taking drugs and all the rest of it. She was only pulling your leg to see how much you'd swallow.'

'Oh, I—I didn't know. Isn't her sister really going to marry a man who's been "inside"?'

'I should think it was extremely unlikely.'

'Then why did Elizabeth say so? Isn't any of it true?'

'I should very much doubt it.'

'But I don't see the point,' protested Sandy. 'I mean, why

tell lies? It's so frightfully silly, apart from anything else.'

'Elizabeth probably doesn't consider that they *are* lies. It amused her to find out just how gullible you are. Her sister's the same. She likes to tell the tale for the devil of it. Neither of them is interested in what is or isn't true so long as it makes a reasonably good story.'

Sandy gave him a quick look. 'I think that's rather awful,' he said. 'You've *got* to trust people. It isn't civilized not to.'

'That's a matter of opinion. It would be an extremely dull world if everyone confined his conversation to the absolute truth—whatever that may be.'

'I don't think so. I think one ought to be able to believe what people say.'

'You do, do you? Then you've got an immense amount of disillusionment ahead of you. I should have thought you'd have learned at school that that sort of thing doesn't pay. As I told you before, you're bound to look a damned fool if you persist in believing everything you're told. Nobody's going to thank you for that. They'll simply think you extremely unsophisticated and incredibly naive.'

The boy got up and looked through the window towards the grey London roofs and the flat featureless buildings. He wished that he were capable of argument, that he could hold on to what seemed straightforward and simple. He did not want to believe that people could set traps to catch his unwary feet : there was no point in it. At school smut was accepted conversation, and funny or not as you chose to think it, but really unpleasant people were sacked. That made sense. His world was not orderly because it was composed of much that lay confused in his mind, but there were portions of it which seemed understandable. There was love for his mother and friendship with Tom Garland. There was the consolation of the Seasons; of blue-white snow on the hills under a wintry sky, of the orchards in spring, and the deep brown fields in autumn when the flocks of birds rose from the furrows with the crisp flutter of wings. And there was the happy sunshine in summer, when he could lie out on the Downs, warm and rested, listening to the contented sheep cropping the dry turf.

He did not want interruption, or a reversal of opinions, or bold changes of outlook. He wanted safety. Other people might seek to rob him of so tame an ambition. His father had been involved in the clamour of destruction in Ireland; he had been part of an Army's occupation in a conquered country; he had sat at tables among men who sought to determine the incidence of war or peace. He was a hard man whose weaknesses were another part of a character which was unable to brook control. Obedience to rule had belonged to his profession and he had subscribed to it out of necessity. It had been a driving force for self-advancement and it had brought him a considerable measure of success.

To the boy he was an enigma. He could not imagine any pleasure in a life which excluded the pursuit of beauty. He was not quite sure what he meant by that, but he sometimes felt that he touched its edge when he saw the sun flush in triumphant farewell the wet fields at evening, or when he read—

> 'Oh! how I love on a fair summer's eve
> When streams of light pour down the golden west,
> And on the balmy zephyrs tranquil rest
> The silver clouds, far, far away to leave
> All meaner thoughts and take a sweet reprieve
> From little cares . . .'*

'What the devil are you mumbling about?'

Sandy stared at his father in hot embarrassment. 'I didn't know I was.'

*John Keats

'Well, what were you saying, anyway?'

'I think I was just remembering some poetry, actually.'

'Holiday task, or something? You'll be telling me next you try to write the stuff yourself. Do you?'

'No.'

'Well, that's something to be thankful for. Don't you ever do anything useful? Seems to me when you stay here, you just lie about watching television. The only time I've ever known you turn it off was when there was a football match on, in which one might reasonably have expected you to take interest. I'm damned if I know what you *are* interested in. You appear to me to be completely devoid of enthusiasm for anything.'

'I like some things.'

'Such as?'

It was impossible to explain that to watch the soaring flight of larks above the Downs gave him a strange excited delight; that a peaceful sea slipping in little waves up the glittering shingle brought him a sense of calm and welcome isolation. He was too ashamed to reveal to anyone so private a lovers' meeting : to his father it would be a piece of hysterical nonsense, utterly to be deplored; to his mother a fatal opportunity for emotional applause, not realizing that even the kindest touch could be an affront. He knew, at least, that all he sought was the poet's 'sweet reprieve from little cares'.

Chapter Four

'THE WIFE,' said Mr Bird, breathing heavily down the tele-phone, 'asked me to say she's sorry she can't come in this morning because the doctor's seen her knee, which is swollen quite bad with water on it. She'll have to lay up a few days, but our Susan'll come round to help you out once we've settled her mother.'

'Poor Mrs Bird! I'm so sorry, and how kind of you to let me know,' said Caroline, 'but are you sure your wife can spare Susan to come to me?'

'It's no trouble,' returned Mr Bird, breathing more gustily than ever, 'seeing the wife's not as you might say in bed. We've got her leg up on a stool and lucky to get her to do that. I reckon Susan will be with you by a quarter past nine.'

'Tell her not to hurry, and take care of your wife as much as she'll let you.'

'I will do, though she don't ever fancy sitting quiet at the best of times.' And with a wheezy chuckle and considerable relief, he rang off.

Caroline, to whom a break in routine was never very welcome, carried a peeled apple and a handful of raisins to the window seat. She disliked the preparation of set meals, but she had taught herself through sheer necessity to be methodical when occasion arose. It seemed to her to be more restful, leaving time to read and, when the sun shone, to wander in her little garden. She knew that she was becoming

45

indolent but she was not in the least ashamed of it. Her needs were few, and she had long drilled herself into an acceptance of an attenuated and ordered life. It had always been her habit to be selective, and to avoid the haste and the untidiness of the short-lived enthusiasm. And if, in the passing of the years, she did not enjoy the solace other women sought in transient friendships and affections, she was not aware of loss. It seemed to her better to maintain a personal belief in what was of value, though the cost was high. To be rewarded for love was in her view only half the story.

If she knew that by refusing the impulse of her heart, she had paid tribute to her spirit long years ago, even now she did not regret it. There was no respect or admiration which she could have given to Alex without sacrifice of principle. Only in secret could she alone know the continuous pain of loving him in the unreason of memory. She was not proud of herself nor did she despise her obduracy, and as she approached the termination of a long uneasy life, she knew that in obedience to her nature she had lived as she herself ordained.

'Excuse me, Miss Chandler.'

Caroline turned from the open window and spent memory, to see a young fresh-faced girl by the door.

'Dad said he spoke about me coming.' The composed little voice was soft. 'On account of Mum's knee.'

'Ah, you're Susan, of course. I do hope Mrs Bird isn't in pain.'

'Not really. It's more uncomfortable than anything else. Dad's taken the prescription down to the chemist to have some tablets made up ... Shall I start on the bedroom, Miss Chandler?'

'Yes, if you will,' said Caroline, and looked at her visitor with approval as she unrolled a clean blue apron and tied

46

it round a neat waist. She was small and slight with an air of quiet efficiency. She had her mother's clear skin and amiable mouth, but her direct glance and firm chin were derived from Mr Bird whose seafaring days had taught him a likeable determination.

'I'll show you where everything is,' Caroline said.

'Mum's told me where to find them,' Susan assured her. 'I'll do your bedroom and the bath while you have your breakfast and read the paper. It's nice about Princess Anne's baby, isn't it?'

Caroline went back to the window seat. She was relieved to find that Mrs Bird's young daughter seemed reliable. She had a pretty smile and a quiet manner. 'I suppose,' Caroline reflected, 'I should be thankful she didn't bring a transistor with her. As a general rule the present-day young live in an atmosphere of strident noise, even when they're at work. I've noticed several shops in the town having their wireless sets turned on while the girls make half-hearted attempts to serve one. I feel so irritable when they expect me to scream with them. Presumably they take it for granted that I'm deaf, which I'm not, though doubtless I have other signs of decrepitude of which I'm unaware. Curiously enough I don't believe young Sandy thought so. Heaven knows what his father would think of me now!'

It seemed a pretty useless sort of speculation and she unfolded the pages of her newspaper rather quickly.

'You'll want some more scouring powder for your bath,' Susan told her, 'if you're ordering on the telephone to-morrow. You're not out of it, but I don't expect they'll send up from the shop till Thursday, and it's nice to have some in hand. I'll wash out your dusters before I go.'

'Sit down and have a cup of tea with me when you've finished.'

'Thank you, Miss Chandler, I will do. I've brought your

47

milk in and made a space for it in the fridge.'

'Good girl.' She could not resist a slight sense of amusement at Susan's composure. Her parents were independent but less self-assured : Caroline remembering the meek approach of the domestic servants of the past, told herself that she preferred the mutual ease of today. She recalled the fair but inflexible discipline exercised by her family over those whom they regarded as the lower orders. They were ordained by God to be privileged, and at no time did they forget it. Her parents had been given to a determined benevolence, spending time and energy on charitable concerns relating to the rescue and prevention of such unfortunates as those who had not always appreciated the efforts made on their behalf, preferring the greater comfort of their regrettable lapses. Half a century later, wars and higher wages had very nearly abolished both the lower grades of domestic service and the necessity to augment earnings with payments for dubious pleasure received. In Caroline's opinion these changes were a sign of a very mild progress. She thought it better not to place undue optimism on the improvement of people in general, but to hope for more restraint among all ages and classes of society. The overspill of emotion, indulgence, or vulgar exploitation, seemed to her a smear which had a tendency to widen. She believed that it bred neglect of human dignity. She clung, not without naivety, to the belief that kindness was a strength, and tenderness a gift to be cherished. And she saw little evidence of either.

She knew that neither her own generation nor those which came after, were often in agreement with her. To risk the condemnation of being 'soft' was to carry the label of weakness and that aroused the contempt of all. Therefore it was better to avoid it. She did not admit, even to herself, that there were times when she wished that she could share her own attitude to those values which seemed to her to throw light upon the dark places of perplexity. But she was growing too old for that : she had walked alone too long to hope to find the sympathy of an unqualified understanding. She knew that she had to do without it until the end of the journey.

'I've given the silver on your dressing table a rub up,' said Susan, 'and if you're going down to the shop or anything, I'll just do this room before I go back home.'

'No,' said Caroline, 'I'm not going out. Don't spend much time on this room today. Your mother polished all the furniture yesteday. I'm going to put the kettle on for our tea now, and I don't like it stewed.'

'Mum told me that. I won't keep you waiting, Miss Chandler.'

When they were seated on either side of the electric fire, Caroline looked at her more closely. The broad childish face was rosy and moist with her exertions. She had washed her small square hands and her hair was tidy. Caroline wondered if she had brought her own comb.

'Have you left school?' she asked. 'Your mother did tell me, but I'm afraid I've forgotten.'

'Yes, I left at Christmas. Of course, I could have gone earlier but I wanted to take my "O" levels before I started work at the hospital.'

'You're going to nurse?'

'That's right. I took first-aid and sewing and cookery because I thought they'd come in useful. And I took English as well because Dad told me Sir Winston Churchill said it was more important than anything. Dad thought the world of him.'

'So did most of us. When do you begin at the hospital?'

'Next month. I'll be eighteen then.'

'And you're looking forward to it?'

'Oh, yes, I've always wanted to nurse.'

'Any particular branch?'

'Well, I'd like to go in for maternity best. Anyway, I'd sooner it was with children than grown-up people.'

'You think they'd be more reasonable? Surely not.'

'Yes, I think I do, if you take them the right way. When my youngest brother had measles he was a young terror, and played poor Mum up till she couldn't do anything with him, but he was ever so good with me right from the start. He knew I wouldn't stand for any nonsense though I wasn't much more than twelve at the time, and we never once had a fight over him taking his medicine. He's a great big chap now, twice the size of me.'

'Girls needs brothers—if they happen to be the right kind,' said Caroline.

'Some's better than others,' said Susan. 'I've got two more, one's in the Fire Service and the other's farming up North, and they're ever such good boys.'

'So your mother told me. She sounds very proud of them.'

'That's right, she is. We're lucky really; you read such things in the papers.'

' "News", Susan, is emphasis in the wrong place.'

'Pardon, Miss Chandler? Well, I get your meaning, but some of it must be true, mustn't it?'

'Of course. But try to keep a sense of proportion.'

She thought afterwards that the Bird family were a very satisfactory sample of healthy English people to whom neither cerebral agitation nor physical excesses proved distractions. They neither sought what they hadn't got, nor applauded those who had more. They were unambitious and simple. The quality which they achieved was contentment rather than happiness. It contained no disturbing element.

She wondered if they were to be envied. To the casual observer, anyhow, there was nothing untidy in their living.

Looking back at her own experience, she was not inclined to believe that she had done anything to be proud of. She had merely eluded deceit. The young flying man who had loved her had failed to persuade her into the falsehood of continuance and that had seemed important to her.

It was another aspect of truth which had caused her to destroy her own happiness and to break with Alex.

On the brink of old age, she still told herself that pride mattered. She knew that for her there would never come a time when cruelty, the evil offspring of unbridled rage, could cease to arouse her anger and her contempt.

And yet, even now, she thought of him as she had first seen him, intrepid, attractive, and determined to break down any resistance that he might encounter. It was the only way in which she could hope to find faith in love.

She had never sought to meet him through all the barren years. He belonged to an insanity of devotion of which she would be the sole spectator. But she walked slowly towards death as a release.

'Well, I'm going now, Miss Chandler,' said Susan at the door. 'I'll be along earlier tomorrow.'

'Give your mother my best wishes.'

'I will do.' The small figure made its way towards the garden gate without haste.

Caroline, watching her, wondered what might be in store for one so young and so self-possessed. It seemed unlikely that she could escape the dangers strewn across her path or elude the unrelenting harshness of life. If her simplicity was her safeguard, it could hardly carry her further than the crumbling wall beyond which the bold waves lashed their invitation. The battle was all ahead of her and not less significant for being unperceived.

Chapter Five

'HAVE YOU any idea what the trouble is?' asked Tom Garland.

'I wish I had,' said Milly with a distracted sigh. 'He just said he didn't want any breakfast and when I reminded him he'd got to fetch the car this morning, he looked on the brink of tears and said he couldn't go. I wonder if I ought to take his temperature?'

'Well, if it will set your mind at rest, I should. If it's normal and he's fit enough, d'you think he'd like me to go with him?'

'Oh, darling, *could* you? I wondered if the fact that he's got to catch a train from here and then change, was upsetting him. He's so shy about asking the way and he's never made this particular journey before. We've always taken him everywhere by car, haven't we? I don't suppose that nice Caroline would think of meeting him, do you?'

'No, darling, I don't, for the excellent reason that there's no good reason why she should,' said Tom comfortably. 'She's probably under the impression that a boy of Sandy's age is perfectly capable of conveying himself across a few miles of the Home Counties unescorted. I feel she is that kind of woman.'

'I suppose,' said Milly wistfully, 'she's quite right.'

'Nobody is entirely right, my pet. We realize, for example,

that any fool can change trains, but that it takes someone of marked originality to travel on the Cornish Express under the impression he was on his way to Godalming.'

'He was only thirteen at the time, Tom.'

'I know. I know. It was our fault for telling him never to look out of the window. I remember thinking at the time that it was a wonderful example of unquestioning obedience.'

'Dear Tom,' said Milly lovingly. Presently she went upstairs to Sandy's room and took his temperature. To their mutual satisfaction he was discovered to be feverish. Milly returned to her husband, looking apologetic. 'A hundred and one,' she said. 'He's had all the ordinary things so perhaps it's just nerves.'

Tom who was used to her method of conveying information, said that they must seek medical advice. 'There are school forms to fill up,' he reminded her, 'which ignore commonsense and maternal experience. We must produce a recognizable disease. I'll ring up Dr Salcombe and ask him to come along.'

'You don't think Sandy's really ill, do you, Tom?'

'Not for a moment. Nor will Salcombe, who is a sensible man. Sandy is a nervous chap and that small mishap with Caroline's garden fence provided him with a golden opportunity to prove what he has always maintained in the teeth of his father's opposition : that driving a car is not for him.'

'Perhaps it's his imagination which tells him that. I do so believe in warnings. I think they're *meant*, if you know what I mean.'

'I also think,' said Tom, 'that being the chap he is, and considerably younger, in more ways than one, than his actual age, he was slightly shaken by his encounter with the young minx Alex saw fit to thrust at him. I've no doubt, my pet, your ex-husband was a libidinous school boy, but Sandy happens to be a very different sort. I shouldn't be surprised

53

when he gets up to Cambridge, if he took to poetry or something of that kind. He'll find his niche, you know, if he's left alone. Well, I suppose I'd better ring up that garage and tell them to deliver his car here.'

'Oh, darling, such an expense!'

Tom grinned. 'Never mind. But, wait a moment, one move at a time. If Dr Salcombe suggests an optician, we'll put Sandy into spectacles, and I'll take it upon myself to inform Alex that, in the circumstances, it will be as well for the boy not to drive at present, and that doubtless he'd like to have the car back to dispose of as he thinks fit. I shouldn't be a bit surprised if he took the opportunity of making a little profit on the sale. With the price of petrol soaring, I rather think he'll let loose a few biting comments and accept my suggestion. All that being so, on second thoughts, I shall not send for the car from Caroline's garage, he can do that for himself.'

'Oh, dear Tom, you are so good and clever,' declared Milly, embracing him, 'I feel so *safe* with you.'

'So you should,' he assured her, 'so you should. That's what I'm here for. Will you ring up Salcombe, or shall I?'

The doctor, a small, portly man, with the cheerful face of a low comedian, and a pair of extremely intelligent, bolting eyes, sat and listened to Sandy's mother and stepfather with the air of having all the time in the world. His sense of humour was more subtle than Tom's and caused some misgiving among his critics.

He was not very popular with his partners owing to their faith in the efficacy of perpetual motion which had the general effect of placing their patients on a conveyor belt.

To the old, Dr Salcombe was unfailingly kind and gentle, to the young and sensitive, he was understanding and patient. If he thought Milly Garland very simple, he liked

54

her none the less for it : he considered Tom a good fellow and considerably more intelligent that he seemed to be. In his opinion, both the Garlands were genuine people who made no attempt to impress anybody. Dr Salcombe found this unusual enough to be interesting. Being unmarried, he was amused by the problems of domesticity and had no preconceived opinions on the upbringing of children.

After examining his patient he returned downstairs and afforded Milly a reassuring and highly unprofessional wink.

'He's all right, m'dear, merely frightened out of his wits by the hazards of the road, plus some totally unnecessary insistence by his father on the temptations of the flesh, which inevitably worked just the other way. Sandy, despite five years at a public school, is still a rather frightened child. Keep him at home for three or four weeks and I'll perjure my immortal soul with a health certificate for his housemaster.'

'I'm in complete agreement with you, but isn't it rather giving way to him?' said Tom.

'Of course,' responded Dr Salcombe cheerfully, 'but I prefer an indulged adolescent to a confused neurotic, and, contrary to accepted opinion, one is not the parent of the other.'

'Does that mean,' asked Milly, slightly bewildered, 'that you agree with me?'

'Of course,' said the little doctor again, closing his bag. 'You will keep that boy at home and tell his father to go to the devil. Sandy's of age, or as near as makes no odds. Until then, you have undisputed custody, and a very reliable support in your husband. And he's good for the boy. I'll look in again on this day week.'

'Oughtn't Sandy to come down to the Surgery?'

'Probably, Mrs Garland, but I see no particular point in

55

his adding a roaring cold, if nothing worse, to his present disorder. I shall come to tea with you to enjoy one of your toasted buns, and to fortify me against an invasion of those who suffer good health so regretfully.'

'I never quite understand Dr Salcombe,' admitted Milly when the portly little figure had trotted down the garden path, 'but I do think he's kind.'

'He's also damned intelligent,' said Tom. 'Most of them imagine they know the lot, in the teeth of the most indisputable evidence to the contrary.'

'What do you think he meant, Tom, about Sandy being worried by Alex talking about sex. I didn't know he had, did you?'

'He may not have done, in so many words. I've a shrewd idea that Alex thinks Sandy too young for his age and rather liked the idea of making him uncomfortable. The chap's a bully, as you know, sweetie, only too well. But there's nothing for you to worry about. With Salcombe's backing, we're on perfectly safe ground. Alex is a bit of a fool as well as everything else. Nothing's more likely to put off a sensitive boy than hurling a brash young party at his head. Dangerous too : it won't happen in Sandy's case, please Allah, but it's one way of encouraging the embryo pansy.'

'Oh, don't! Of course, some of them are quite nice to meet, but I do wish the Church wouldn't talk about it as if it didn't matter.'

'Darling, don't *worry*! The prevalent mood at the moment is to make out that we're all too understanding and broad-minded—whatever that may mean—to be disturbed by any departures from conventional behaviour. It makes us feel extremely continental, and applauded members of the Common Market.'

56

'*Does* it?' said Milly, looking very surprised.

Tom hugged her. 'Of course it does. Personally I consider it slightly deplorable, but never mind. Tell me, do you think it would be a good idea if we kept hens?'

'In the old stables? Do you think they'd lay?'

'Good heavens, yes. They'd wake us up at dawn, laying like mad. Think of it, fresh eggs for breakfast every morning. Plus bacon, of course . . . That's an idea, we might keep a pig.'

'Oh, darling, I think I'd rather not. It would be so sad to have to kill it.

'I couldn't agree more. They tend to die loudly. Pigs, ruled out. We'll dig for victory instead.'

'Victory?'

'Against the demands of the Common Market.'

'But I thought . . .'

'Don't, my pet. It confuses both of us. I shall buy a couple of large spades tomorrow. Make a list of your favourite vegetables, excluding the more exotic, and I will request the Army & Navy Stores to supply me with half-a-dozen books containing coloured plates of tastefully arranged leeks lying on a bed of furiously blushing beetroot. We might even win prizes at the local shows. I can't imagine why we didn't think of it before.'

'You had your horses, darling.'

'Ah! Then I was young and carefree.'

'You only gave them up, Tom dear, a couple of years ago.'

'Is it so short a time since we nearly went bust? The secret of a contented nature really lies in the judicious cultivation of forgetfulness.'

She looked at him with customary admiration. He put things so well! And he was never out of humour. She hoped that Sandy might be influenced by so much optimism.

57

'I don't know what I should have done without you,' she said.

'What a very pleasant reflection. Neither do I. Though why you should look as if you were about to cry, I don't know. You have the most original way of expressing delight.'

'I can't help it, Tom.'

'Of course you can't, floods of tears should always be entirely spontaneous and quite inappropriate. Let's go upstairs and play silly card games with Sandy.'

Caroline, watching her little pear tree drop white petals upon the drenched grass, felt unaccountably depressed. All the new life which was emerging from the warm wet ground, failed to elate her. The cycle of the seasons seemed to have a relentless regularity which brought no answering delight. She was no more, she told herself, than a spectator of such things as had once afforded her a joyous sense of participation. Now she belonged nowhere and to no one.

It was absurd, she knew, to resent the fact of loneliness : only yesterday and the days which went before, she had told herself that her solitary state was not to be deplored, and usually her common sense was constant.

But there had returned to her something of past turmoil and dark distress. The intrusion of the boy, Sandy, so unlike Alex and yet in some indefinable way, faintly resembling him, clutched at her heart. Some movement of his long hands, some intentness of his glance, some trick of voice, all momentary and quickly lost, had startled her into the pain of stirred memory. She shrank from the exhaustion of roused feeling. It could have no reality. Unexpectedly she felt strangely lonely. She wanted, she told herself, to get away to some safe place of refuge in her mind where she could be assailed by no more suffering. But she knew it was not true. She had outlived all physical longing, but the emptiness

58

of living came back to her and the thrust of senseless sorrow. No amount of tortuous self-argument could prove to her that she could overcome a love which had been so irresistibly cruel a companion throughout the silent years.

Chapter Six

'WHERE THE BLAZES is my tie?'

'Where you left it, on the back of the chair.'

Alex, before the cheap little dressing table, fastened his collar: he looked out of temper. 'Why don't you get yourself a better room?'

The girl on the bed stretched her arms lazily. 'Why should I? What's the matter with this one? I've not had the divan long. A friend gave it to me. It was reduced from ever such a lot in the sales: he was in that line himself; he was ever such a nice boy but he went on his holidays last summer and got off with a girl on the roller-skating rink ... well, I say *girl*, I bet she'll never see twenty-five again. He showed me her photo when they got married: I don't wonder she had her back turned ... you know, looking over her shoulder and grinning ... silly fool. Him, I mean.'

'I've no doubt you consoled yourself adequately.'

'You bet I did. I don't waste my time ... where are you off to?'

'My club. You'd better get yourself those new slippers you were talking about.'

'What's the hurry? ... Oh, thanks a lot ... you haven't got separate notes, I don't suppose? Last time I tried to change a fiver on the bus, the driver was downright cheeky.'

'How much was the fare?'

'About ten p.'

'Why didn't you walk?'

'That's a good one! I'd done a couple of perms that afternoon, and been on my feet all day. Oh, ta . . . you know I hate looking conspicuous. Do you like my fringe?'

'No.'

'Oh, why *not*? Everyone else does.'

'That's why. Elsie, I must bolt.'

'I don't see why you want to rush off. You never stop, do you?'

'Never.' His smile was half-irritable, half-amused. Because his figure was still trim and his lean brown face not more worn than was becoming, he liked to think that he concealed his years.

'You know what you are,' she said, 'you're a tease! You're not a bit nice to me really.'

'Now don't whine, I hate it.'

'I wasn't. It's just that you're so sort of funny,' she explained. 'Still you wouldn't come back if you didn't like me. What are you looking for now?'

'A cigarette.'

'Here you are. I'll get up if you like.'

'Well, put something on.'

She slipped a silk vest over her rumpled fair head and pulled up a pair of black tights. 'Shall we see if there's something nice on the telly?'

'What the devil for?'

'All right. I only asked. Why are you so cross?'

'Aren't I always?'

She looked at him warily. 'No, you can be nice when you try.'

He said nothing and she decided to hold her tongue. After all, a girl took a chance with a chap of his age. Some of her friends at work warned her that Alex was no sugar daddy.

'You mind out, Elsie,' they said. 'What do you want with him, anyway?'

She was not quite sure. The slight sensation of fear, which was something to do with it, excited her. He was quite unlike the boys who had lured her into the empty huts on the recreation ground, or the tearaway lads who carried her on the backs of their motor bicycles to the common after dark. She was very popular with the boys. She often told herself that if Mum and Dad knew what she was up to, they would have a couple of fits. But what did it matter? She knew how to take care of herself. And when her parents moved into a council flat, she struck out and took a room above a dress shop, whose decorative owner had her own life to lead and never worried so long as she got her rent regularly.

'Suits me,' said Elsie.

Her independence amused Alex. He had come across her when she was employed in a tobacconist's shop, but she soon transferred herself to a hairdresser's establishment where the work was much more agreeable. 'I can doll myself up a bit and get the girls to give me a few bits and pieces, left-overs and that,' she assured herself.

Her friends were always telling her to be careful. 'He's not the sort you want to take risks with,' they said, 'when they're getting on they can turn nasty.'

She put it down to jealousy: he wore an Army tie that wasn't a fake, and well-fitting suits. 'He talks posh, too,' said Elsie. She wished he would take her out in his car but he never did. He just came to see her at the week-end when he was sure of finding her alone.

'I wish we could go down to the sea on Sunday,' she said.

'Then you must get some of your friends to take you.'

'I meant you and me.'

'That's not exactly a bright idea, I'm afraid.'

She wished that he wouldn't frown; he looked harsh and

forbidding. She had tried once, without permission, to call him by his first name, and his sudden explosion of anger had really frightened her.

'I'm sorry,' she had faltered, 'I didn't know you'd mind.'

'Well, I do.'

'What do I call you then?'

'Need you say anything?'

'It seems so funny not to.'

His annoyance faded. 'Say Major Orme if it makes you any happier. But don't mention it to anyone else. Is that clear? I strongly object to girls who kiss and tell.'

'I never would.'

'Well, don't forget.'

She comforted herself with the reflection that she had never told the girls at the shop anything beyond the fact that she had a friend who had been something important at the War Office before he retired from the Army, and was both older and grander than anyone they knew. Distinctly nettled they said she was welcome to him.

'Jealous, that's what they are,' decided Elsie. And watching him as he laced up his shoes, she said : 'You will come next Saturday, won't you?'

'I expect so.'

'I do miss you. It seems ever such a long week. I wish I didn't have to wait so long.'

'We've been into that already.'

'The girl I share this place with—well, I'm her tenant really—goes out every night. *I* could if I liked, but I only go to the pictures nowadays if there's other girls going too.'

'Given the circumstances, that's a sensible sort of precaution.'

'I—I thought you'd be pleased.'

'Oh, hell, I *am* pleased, you little fool. What do you expect me to say? Are you trying to tell me you want some

63

more nylons? If so, nothing doing.'

Tears rolled down her cheeks. 'Oh, you are horrid . . . you know I don't.'

'I know you're being extraordinarily exasperating . . . Now stop it, unless you want me to give you something to cry about. Do you?'

'No.'

'Then behave yourself.'

It occurred to him later when he went away that she had looked genuinely startled. He remembered his wife, Milly, had been just as lacking in gumption. Of late years he had usually avoided young girls in favour of older sophisticated women, who were hard and well-off and capable of entertaining him in the way he preferred. Occasionally he suspected them of taking some kind of advantage of him, but he was not quite sure what it was. Once or twice he had stumbled when he was dancing, and, recovering immediately, glanced at the face of his partner to catch, if he were not much mistaken, a covert look of amusement. Well, that one was fifty if she was a day, with every known aid to give the illusion of youth : perfect clothes and all the rest of it, but what she had got to crow about, he didn't know. Curious that he should feel so low in spirit since he had left young Elsie and her tearful plaints.

He felt fed up with himself; in the past the ignominy of depending for amusement upon so inexperienced a girl would have seemed unthinkable. But, for one reason or another, he seemed to have lost a good many of the friends who had shown him hospitality in the past. He was assured that people were not so easy to get on with as they used to be. At his Club he often seemed to find acrimony; it was more difficult than it used to be to make up a four at bridge; he was seldom a member of a theatre party, and when he was invited out to dinner, he never met anyone who really took interest in him.

It was a fact that he had often made enemies in the past, but he was surprised that people should have such long memories. He was soured by the reflection that so many of his friends had chosen to lose sight of him. It was, of course, all part and parcel of the indifference of the age. Nothing was as good as it used to be.

'I feel rotten,' he muttered. 'I'll have a drink and turn in.'

He was just out of his bath when the telephone rang and not pleased to be dragged from a comfortable sense of relaxation.

'Yes, who is it?'

'Is that you, Orme? It's Garland here.'

'Who?'

'Garland. Milly's husband. We felt you ought to know young Sandy isn't very fit, and our doctor thinks he ought to miss at least a part of the coming term.'

'Why, what's the matter with him?'

'Nothing very serious. Apparently he's more or less outgrown his strength and is rather anaemic and under weight. He's got to have his eyes tested next week and he's been ordered fresh air, plenty of rest and no strain.'

'What the devil does that mean? His mother has always been a fool about him.'

'I don't in the least agree. She's an excellent mother.'

'That's a matter of opinion. Anyhow, what has it got to do with me?'

'Nothing. But we thought you might like to adjust the matter of the school fees which you normally pay. They'll probably let you off anyhow a part of the term if he doesn't get back for some weeks. Incidentally there's a slight bill for expenses at a garage : he drove his car into a fence and knocked it about a bit. I don't mind settling the account if you'd rather not. By the way, he'll be eighteen in a fort-

65

C

night's time won't he, and therefore legally of age?'

'Anyone more incapable of being considered mature, I can't imagine.'

'It happens to be the law. Well, anyhow, we thought we'd let you know how things were.'

'Best thing he can do is to go back to school.'

'The doctor thinks otherwise. He's a sound chap and knows his job.'

'Briefed, no doubt, by Milly. Well, if that's all, I won't stay here listening to you any longer.' He rang off abruptly and returned to the heat of the bathroom. 'Damn waste of time,' he told his lathered reflection in the shaving mirror. He no longer decided that he felt ill; he would dress and go to the Club. He was bound to find two or three fellows who would give him a game.

'The man's an even greater ass than I remember,' he reflected, 'he probably gives in to Milly the whole dam' time. I never met a stupider woman. If Garland hadn't defended her treatment of the boy, he wouldn't have turned out a nervous little wreck. Between the pair of them they've made a complete mess of the fellow.'

And he felt more exasperated than ever. It infuriated him to realize that Sandy didn't like him, and the recognition made him aware that there was nothing he could do about it. He still remembered the few blistering lines Tom Garland had sent him before the divorce, nor was it any consolation that violence had been kept out of the evidence, of course, entirely for their own ends. There was no question of their jeopardizing his case by confusing the issue. They were determined to get rid of him. The force with which he had flung Milly against the wall had done more than bruise her forehead and shake her plump little body, it had destroyed the last remnant of any feeling she had once had for him. And he knew it. He thought it unfair; other women put up

66

with far worse things. In the cold silence of the Garlands' resistance against him, he remained helpless. Throughout the succeeding years, in the sour bitterness of anger, nothing had healed so rank an insult. The half-sentimental, half-contemptuous feeling he had once had for his wife, based upon a belief in her original feeling for him, had shrivelled and died before her determined unforgiveness. It defeated his imagination : he could not see himself in any light but his own.

Going into his study, he mixed another drink. What was it that fellow Garland had said about Milly, *an excellent mother*? He had never heard such balderdash in all his life.

'I'm going out,' he said aloud, and left his untouched whisky on the table. His forehead felt hot and he had an absurd sense of finding his own company insupportable. He dialled directory enquiries. Sandy had told him the name of Caroline's cottage in the country. Well, there was no harm in getting hold of her number ... He wondered what she would say if he rang her up after all these years; odd to think that she was an ageing woman now : she had infuriated him once : there was no blinking the fact that she had made a fool of him. He had never been able to shrug that off. The amazing thing was he could have sworn that she loved him. It was ridiculous to suppose that he hadn't meant anything to her. The next time would have been all right, he had been absolutely certain of that. Obviously he would have had to get tough with her. He had given way to her long enough. But there had been no next time. All that had happened between then and his marriage had been the usual cycle of casual affairs, too familiar to be recalled. If Milly had not had money, he wouldn't have given her a second thought : an amiable woman with a gentle nature was hardly in his line. But naturally all that was a good thing in a wife with an income of her own. And he had not,

67

he considered, been more than reasonably annoyed when she became pregnant. But, after the baby, frail and tiny, was born, he felt cheated. It was hardly to be expected that a man who had never been ill in his life, would have watched, with any degree of satisfaction, a delicate child become his mother's sole absorption. That was what had started the rot : after that he had spent less and less of his leave at home, becoming more and more irritable until his control had slipped and he had hurled poor little Milly, squealing, across the room.

He sometimes wondered what Caroline would have done if it had happened to her. He didn't see *her* weeping and rushing into another man's arms.

'No harm, I suppose, after all this time, in looking her up,' he muttered. 'I'll have to settle Sandy's blasted bill at the garage and make arrangements about getting the car. It's the deuce of a nuisance but it can't he helped. That boy's such a fool.'

He drove through half-empty streets into the quiet suburbs. They depressed him horribly : small shuttered shops gave way to closed factories, to flats with blank windows, to little villas with narrow strips of garden.

England's ruined, he told himself; there were no fine houses in beautiful parks, no symptoms of affluence and hospitality. 'Of course, I'm looking in the wrong place,' he amended, 'it's hardly likely Caroline could afford anything better than a cottage on the fringe of a country town. Though why she prefers that to a small flat in a civilized city, Heaven alone knows.'

He consulted a map twice before he came to what he was looking for. The Spring evening was growing grey, wet trees hung heavy branches moving uneasily in the teasing wind. He stopped the car and opened the door. There was no one about. A few neat little houses stood between trim

68

hedges : a tortoiseshell cat sat, asleep, on a window ledge. He looked for a label on a gate and got out slowly. He stretched his legs and half wished that he had not come. His head ached, he was aware of being very tired, and his cold hands felt clumsy.

Behind him came the sound of light, slightly uneven footsteps, the tread of an elderly woman. He turned and heard a quiet voice say : 'Were you coming to see me, Alex?'

Her tone was a little deeper and older than he remembered, and when he looked at her, he saw that she no longer held herself proudly, and that from her spare face the aroused colour was slowly ebbing.

'As a matter of fact, I was,' he said. 'I hear you were kind to my boy. I wanted to thank you. And to make arrangements to collect the car.'

'He's a nice fellow,' she said, and led the way to the house. The little cat slipped off the window-sill and into a neighbouring garden. She settled down among the roots of a lilac bush, and remained watchful.

'She's shy,' said Caroline, as they went into the hall.

'Mutual antipathy,' he said, and added, because it didn't seem a very good start : 'How are you?'

'Growing old. Aren't we all?'

'You live alone?'

'I do.'

'From force of circumstances or inclination?'

She looked amused. 'I could say both. Will you have some sherry?'

'I'd love some.' He watched her more closely as she moved about the room. 'Sandy told me you look patient. What d'you think of that?'

'I hope it's true.' She put his drink beside him and added : 'Do you find it too warm in here?'

'Well, it's a bit heavy this evening. We're probably going to have thunder.'

She pushed open a window. 'Then let's have some fresh air.'

'Thank you,' he said. His hand shook a little as he raised his glass. 'Well, here's to you, Caroline ... Incidentally, it's an absurdly long time since we met. I feel very flattered that you recognized me.'

'It wasn't difficult.'

'You heard about my divorce, of course?'

'Yes, I'm sorry.'

'I can't say I was. What did you think of Sandy?'

'I liked him.'

'Not much like me, is he?'

'Mentally, I should say not at all,' returned Caroline. 'His long legs reminded me of you, and his way of dropping his head and watching one when he's listening.'

'Good heavens, did I do that? You've got an incredible memory.' He looked pleased. 'Well, what have you been doing with yourself? Do you ever go abroad nowadays?'

'No.'

'Why not?'

'Too tiring.'

'Don't you get bored living on your own?'

'One can feel extraordinarily bored with the wrong people.'

'Need they necessarily be the wrong ones?'

'You're asking a lot of questions, aren't you?' said Caroline.

She did not expect him to apologize. He was frowning as though he were puzzled.

'What an odd sort of life you must lead,' he said.

'It suits me. Incidentally, did you come to see me for any particular reason?'

'Is that a hint for me to go?'

'No ... of course not.'

'My excuse was to pay for Sandy's confounded car and to tell the garage to sell it for me.'

'Doesn't he want it?'

'I shouldn't think so,' he returned. 'Anyhow, I see no point in his having one at present if he's such a dam' bad driver.'

'Is he?'

'He told his mother he hates driving, and until he acquires more sense, I see no particular reason why I should foot his bills.'

'Did he want to have a car in the first place?' asked Caroline.

'I suppose he told you he didn't?'

'I forget. It didn't make much impression on me if he did.'

'You just found it necessary to take his part.' His face grew dusky red, but instead of adding a biting retort, he covered his eyes and was silent.

'Are you all right, Alex?'

'Yes ... I felt slightly giddy, that's all. It came on a little before. It's nothing.'

'Well, sit still for a while and don't bother to talk.'

'I told you, it's nothing. Look here, let's go and dine somewhere, quietly.' The dark colour was fading, leaving his thin face mottled. 'Too much high-life,' he said with a half-sly, half-sheepish grin. He wondered if she had heard him since she showed no evidence of interest. She might, he thought, at least have looked amused. He had never been able to tell what she was thinking.

'Tonight?'

'Obviously. Why not?'

'Like this?'

'Of course. Nobody dresses on a Sunday evening. Anyhow, it's a very becoming get-up. Don't make difficulties. Don't you want to come?'

'Yes,' she said, and laughed a little. 'I'd like to, very much.'

'Good. I was afraid you were expecting me to coax you, but I didn't believe that you'd forgotten all expertise to that extent.'

'I never had any. I'll just go and arrange myself ... The bathroom's at the end of the corridor.'

'Thank you. Caroline?'

'Yes?'

'Nothing.'

He looked very worn, she thought, his chin sharpened and the little hollows she remembered beneath his cheekbones longer and deeper. In her room she combed her hair and repaired her face with a sense of regret. The wasted years, before the bloom of youth finally left her, had once made her heart ache. She was too tired now to recall the weight of sorrow which she had carried. There had been no dedication in her life, nothing which made demands upon her, which expected her at least to share a part of the world's burden. She had stood aside, in the shade while the hot sun burned those who challenged its rays : she had given and taken nothing that mattered. She had looked for a way out of the confusion which had destroyed her happiness, and as the uneventful years slipped by, ceased even to try to school herself into acceptance of pain.

But now shocked into a realization of the unexpected, pulled out of the seclusion of protective immunity, she was at once elated and shaken. There was nothing to be won, life had no recognizable gift for her. She felt bewildered.

She went back to her living-room and saw him standing by the open window, looking at the swaying trees still lit by the pale gold of the fading sun.

'What do you do with yourself all day?' he asked as he

led the way out to his car.

'Very little. I do some rather unenterprising gardening, and I occasionally baby-sit to give an exhausted young mother a chance to have an evening out with her husband.'

'Good heavens, why do that?'

'Why not? They're a nice little couple, and Rosie, the small daughter's sweet.'

'Sandy used to yell his head off if he was left with a stranger. Milly, of course, gave way to him, and then complained that, when I had any leave, I spent it in a less vocal atmosphere.'

'He was very delicate, wasn't he?'

'I suppose so. He was terrified of me for some reason. By the way, where are we making for?'

'I believe the Crown's quite good.'

'What do you mean, you *believe*? Don't you know?'

'People say it is.'

'Where *do* you usually go?'

'Nowhere.'

'Why?'

'Habit, I suppose. I like staying at home.'

'Doing what?'

'Reading, chiefly.'

'Don't you watch television?'

'A little ... If we're going to the Crown, it's about a couple of miles beyond the town.'

'You wouldn't rather go further afield?'

'No, I don't think so.'

'Don't you ever get sick of the country?'

'No. I'm very fond of it. It's so lovely for the greater part of the year.'

'But tame.'

'Possibly.'

'And you don't mind that?'

'No.'

'Is your brother still alive?'

'Oh, yes. He's retired but he clings to Cambridge, and an admirable couple who look after him.'

'And you broke away?'

'I prefer Sussex.'

'And your own company?'

'Yes.'

'Why?'

'It happens to suit me. My brother is a little cantankerous to live with, and the wrong person only accentuates—other things.'

'That isn't what you began to say,' he declared as he drove into the inn's courtyard.

The little dining-room contained a few sedate couples wearing their Sunday best with an air of appropriate discomfort.

'Do you still go to church, Caroline?' he asked, as they sat down.

'Sometimes.'

A young untidy waiter regarded them with a cynical eye. They seemed to him likely to prove indifferent clients. Neither ate with much appreciation, and if the gentleman drank a good deal of brandy, it did not appear to improve his spirits.

'What always puzzles me,' said Alex, presently, 'is why you ran away.'

She was silent; the question seemed superfluous.

'Why did you, Caroline? What were you frightened of?'

'Need we go into all that now?'

'Yes. I want to know. I can't believe that you were such an arrant little coward as to be afraid of me.'

'I was afraid,' she said slowly, 'of myself, that I might

come to think cruelty didn't matter.'

'Oh, *that*,' he said with contempt, 'all the fuss simply because I happened to lose my cool. The pony was a nervous little beast, I got rid of him soon after. I was sorry about your spaniel, but I don't suppose he was really hurt.'

'He had two broken ribs.'

'Did he really? Well, as I say, I'm sorry, but it was his own fault for getting in the light. Oh, for Heaven's sake, Caroline, you don't want to go over all that, after all this time.'

'No. But you asked me a question. And I gave you a truthful answer.'

'You thought me cruel? Well, I can tell you this, I've never been guilty of premeditated cruelty in my life. Possibly at school I may have been, well, much the same as most people.'

'I think I'd rather not hear, Alex.'

'All right, I'm not suggesting that I was ever brutal to anyone. Women don't understand that sort of thing. When I was at Sandhurst . . .'

'As you say,' she interrupted, 'some women, anyhow, don't understand that sort of thing. I happen to be one of them. Alex, if you're driving me back, don't you think you'd better go slow with that brandy?'

'Are you suggesting that I'm getting tight?'

'Yes.'

'Milly would never have dared even to hint at that.'

'Did she have cause?'

'No, as a matter of fact, she didn't.' His laugh was short. 'Forget her.'

'Can you?'

'Of course.'

'Isn't that a little hard on Sandy?'

'Not in the least. Why should it be?'

'After all,' suggested Caroline, 'she's his mother.'

'All right, but she elected to clear out and look after the child. Good heavens, you're not taking her part, are you?'

'I'm not taking anyone's part.'

He looked at her. 'Would you have played her game if you'd been in her shoes?'

'I don't know any of the facts, do I?'

He moved in sudden exasperation and sent his glass crashing to the ground. The young waiter hurried forward to gather up the broken pieces and stem the little stream of brandy.

'Bring me another,' said Alex. He was dusky red.

'Is that strictly necessary?' murmured Caroline.

He paid no attention. 'My eyes have been bothering me lately,' he said, 'things look blurred for some reason. It's very irritating.'

'Have you had them tested?'

'No. It's probably liver. Are you going abroad this summer ... no, you said you weren't ... I forgot. We—we must do this again some time soon, Caroline. Why we left it so long, I can't imagine. Oh, hell, I've forgotten to call at the garage about the boy's car.'

'I'll do it for you tomorrow.'

'Will you? Tell them to post the bill to me.'

'And you really want them to sell the car?'

'What? Oh, yes, yes, of course. I'll ring them up. Thank you, Caroline. It's been nice seeing you.'

'You'll drive back carefully, won't you?'

'Nervous?'

'I was thinking of your going up to London.'

'Don't worry.' He finished his drink, sighed and looked a little amused. 'I shan't get run in for being tight, if that's what you're worrying about. D'you want me to take you back now?'

'Yes, please.'

By the time he reached London, he had forgotten Elsie and her pretty ways. It had been going on long enough, anyway. If he was feeling off-colour, she was no use to him. But Caroline understood him. He could have a friendship with her. He didn't want sex and the demands of youth. There wasn't much point in keeping up a sense of grievance because of what happened years ago. He was prepared to be magnanimous. He sat down in an easy chair with a sense of self-satisfaction. It was probably time he took things quietly. Anyhow for a while. He felt sleepy and closed his eyes.

'What an odd sort of life you must lead ...'

'It suits me ...'

Chapter Seven

THE LONG unkind Spring had given place to a sudden golden warmth, delayed Summer came to the leafy woods, to the gratified fields where blackbirds and thrushes sang happy psalms, to the gardens where murmuring bees clung to the ravaged flowers.

'It's high time I was on me legs again,' said Mrs Bird.

'You'll do as the doctor says an' give yourself another week,' declared Mr Bird, 'there's no call to spoil the ship for a ha'pennyworth of tar.'

'And when I *do* get around I expect I'll find everything put away in the wrong place; tidy isn't in it! That's you all over.'

'I reckon me and Susan haven't done so bad. You wouldn't have liked it if we hadn't left you something to grumble over, now would you?'

Mrs Bird permitted herself a slow indulgent smile. She was much attached to her husband, whom she treated with a resigned patience, believing all men to be creatures of inferior understanding.

'I reckon Miss Chandler 'll be pleased to see me back,' she said. 'I daresay Susan's done all right, but when you've worked for someone as long as I have, you get to know their ways, and you don't have to be told every little thing. Miss Chandler isn't what I'd call domestic, but she'd soon notice if the Laundry hadn't sent back her sheets folded nice, or if the milkman didn't call on his usual day to be paid. She's not one to run up bills and there's plenty call themselves ladies never give a thought to that.'

'Mebbe she has to be careful herself,' said Mr Bird. 'I don't fancy she's got much. She don't dress like it.'

'She dresses very suitable and plain,' retorted Mrs Bird. 'Real ladies never look showy. You don't know nothing about it.'

'Reckon that's a fact. I only meant she dresses nice and quiet—like you.'

'Well, of course,' said Mrs Bird, mollified, 'me being rather on the stout side and Miss Chandler a lot taller and thinner, she can't pass nothing of hers on to me seein' it wouldn't fit. But I don't fancy neither of us wants to be thought what you might call smart.'

'Suits me,' he assured her, 'always has, always will ... Here's Susan. You're early, girl.'

Their daughter, a little breathless and flushed, joined them and sat down on a chair with a long sigh. 'It's got hot all of a sudden,' she said.

Her mother gave her a quick look. 'What did you have for your dinner?'

'The same as they did,' Susan told her. 'Cold lamb and a salad. And Miss Chandler said I was to finish up the stewed apples and cream.'

'What about her, then?' asked Mrs Bird. 'Didn't she want none? I don't wonder she's s'thin.'

'They had biscuits and cheese,' said Susan uncertainly.

'Who's "they"?' asked her mother sharply. 'It's not often she has company for lunch.'

'She'd a gentleman with her—round about her age I'd say—put me in mind of old Colonel Brown that leads off the British Legion on Remembrance Sunday, only—only not the same.'

Mr Bird chuckled. 'Never seen a shot fired in anger, he hasn't, poor old soul.'

'Get the girl a drink of water,' interrupted Mrs Bird. 'She's tired and there's no call for her to wait for her tea, considerin' the time it takes you to make it. Go on, now, look sharp.' And when he went off grumbling a little, for he disliked being made to hurry when he didn't know the reason for it, she frowned at her daughter in perplexed concern. 'What's the matter, duck?'

'Her friend didn't speak nice at all,' said Susan in tearful indignation. 'Not the way a gentleman should, when Miss Chandler was out of the room a moment.'

'He never touched you?' demanded her mother sharply. 'He didn't lay a finger on you, did he?'

'No, he didn't, but I was frightened he was going to because of the way he looked, so I went round the table towards the door. And he spoke dreadful, and then Miss Chandler come back and I went over to the kitchen and changed my shoes and come back home. I don't want to work there, Mum, not if he was to be there again, I don't.'

'Well, there's no call to cry because I wouldn't let you. I'll be back there meself Monday, and Dad can take a message over tomorrow to say you're not feeling well. Some old gentlemen don't know how to behave themselves and that's a fact. You'd better not say too much to your father else he might offer to knock his block off. I wonder where he come from, anyway. Not round here I reckon.'

'He'd a car outside her house,' said Susan wiping her eyes. 'Oh, Mum, you are lovely to me!'

'All right, give us a kiss and cheer up. Miss Chandler did ought to be more careful who she leaves about the place. Dirty old man! Don't you think about it no more, it's over and done with.'

Mr Bird, dispatched on his bicycle after his midday meal

to deliver his wife's message, looked extremely annoyed. He did not like his mission, feeling that it was more Mrs Bird's business than his, but he was very fond of his young daughter and any threat to her serenity angered him. He was a straightforward man and his rules of conduct were uncomplicated. Having heard from Mrs Bird that Susan had been affronted by something Miss Chandler's visitor had said to her, his sense of delicacy was affronted. Things happened, he reminded himself, to other people's children. For him, she was still the clear-eyed child who wound her arms round his neck when she kissed him goodnight. Nor was he far wrong. The home in which they had nurtured her was the place in which they had sought to keep at bay all squalor and falsity, and her trust in them was the measure of their reward.

Warm from his ride uphill and from honest indignation, Mr Bird propped his bicycle against Caroline's hedge, mopped his face and walked towards the gate. He was relieved to see that there was no car in the lane. 'I mightn't be able to trust meself,' he muttered as he walked up the cobbled path.

He was a good deal discomfited, however, to see Caroline sitting in a basket chair on the porch, before he had had time to make up his mind what to say. He thought that she looked a little anxious as she glanced up, but she only said quietly : 'Ah! Mr Bird. I hear that your wife will be able to come back on Monday. I'm so glad she is better.'

'She's pretty fair : the doctor says she can please herself about coming back, but he'd sooner she didn't do no kneeling . . . I've come for Susan's apron.'

'She's not returning? In that case, I must give you her money.'

'Yes, well, it's only two days to the end of the week and I'll bring your vegetables in for Sunday, same as usual.

Susan's not feeling very well.' And because Caroline had nothing to comment on that, he felt a sudden spasm of anger. 'The gentleman you had here come after her and frightened her ... He'd no business to speak as he did to a decent girl ... Her mother got her to repeat what he said and there was no doubting what he was after. Our Susan's little more than a child when all's said and done ... An' I'm not having her coming here to work again; I'm sorry to have to say it, but I reckon you'd feel the same way if she was your daughter.'

Caroline was opening her bag. 'Let me see, she was paid by the week, wasn't she, like her mother? So this time it's one week less two days. Will you give it to Susan? And tell Mrs Bird I shall be glad to see her on Monday.'

'And never a word of what you might call apology,' he told his wife later; 'she looked sort of white, and spoke a bit cold and kind of saw me off the premises as you might say—well, as far as the gate anyway.'

'Well, I daresay she felt awkward,' explained Mrs Bird. 'I reckon she's used to nice manners and mebbe she put two and two together when Susan run off home. I wonder who he was? I've never seen anyone at Miss Chandler's place, bar her few friends, and there's no gentlemen among them so far as I know. Well, perhaps she'll tell me more on Monday.'

'Perhaps she won't,' said Mr Bird darkly.

His wife paid no attention. She was not normally a demonstrative woman, but to her family her attachment was inarticulate and profound. The thought of injury to any of them roused her anger, and for her young daughter she had special feeling. She had no particular sympathy with the young, but it seemed to her that she had gone the right way about things with her children. Mr Bird, having taken off his belt more than once to his boys, had undoubtedly won their respect, and their youngest child had never given them any trouble; she supposed they had been soft with Susan, but she had always shown so much good sense and understanding that Mrs Bird felt an unconfessed pride in her little daughter.

'I reckon we've brought her up right,' she told herself.

It was this reflection which sustained her when she confronted Caroline on Monday morning. Mr Bird hadn't had the courage to speak out to Miss Chandler : that was men all over, they always left everything to the women. Mrs Bird, giving an extra firm twist to her apron string, went into the living-room with Caroline's breakfast tray, and answered enquiries about the state of her leg with unusual shortness.

'You mustn't stand more than is strictly necessary, and, remember, there must be no kneeling at present.'

'Very good 'm.'

'Has your doctor given you a tonic?'

'Yes 'm. It's not the same as Mr Bird brought me back last time. It's more of a mixture : the other was tablets ... Miss Chandler?'

'Yes?'

'About Susan kind of walking out so sudden ... not that I blame her ... she's a good girl, though I say so, and that's the way she's been brought up. Her father and me have taught her what's right. And,' added Mrs Bird, very flushed and hurried, 'we didn't reckon that if she came to work here, while I was taken bad, that she'd have been treated the way she was ... followed her round the table he did, saying what he'd no business to, trying to catch a hold of her, an' when she kind of dodged him, he spoke out quite disgraceful. She never gave him no encouragement, she wouldn't, she's not like that, not being scarcely more than a child, as you might say.'

'I'm sorry, Mrs Bird. I can quite understand that you were distressed.'

'Yes, well, we both was. Susan don't cry easy but she'd had a shock. You'll pardon my asking if he lives anywhere around here. There's more strangers than there used to be in the old days, and plenty bad characters too, I daresay.'

'No. He lives in London : he is an old friend of mine, whom I hadn't seen for many years. I will take care that this doesn't occur again. I promise you that. He is a retired Army officer and you need have no anxiety about her meeting him again.'

'Yes, well, so I should hope. I'm sorry, Miss Chandler, but I don't think there's much of the officer and a gentleman about acting like that, nor speaking so rude.'

'I have already apologized for what happened, and given you an assurance that it will not happen again. It is possible that Susan quite unwittingly exaggerated the whole episode . . .'

'Pardon me, Miss Chandler, she did not. She heard what he said as clear as I'm speaking to you; and it was him trying to get a hold of her . . .'

'But she avoided him, so there is the possibility of a mistake, isn't there? . . .'

'Excuse me, there is not. Real frightened she was. It's a good thing my eldest boy wasn't at home . . .'

'Mrs Bird, believe me I understand how you feel but no harm has come and I think we should try to forget all this. You must trust me to see that there is no possibility of such a thing happening again. And now do you think you could prepare the salad for my lunch? You can do that sitting down, can't you?'

She hoped that the relationship between them of mutual goodwill had not been spoiled. Mrs Bird was still looking very much affronted. What a fool Alex had been! Of course, the girl was as fresh-faced and innocently attractive as only extreme youth could render her, and if he had only wanted a snatched kiss or two and a hug, one could hardly blame him. The risk of getting caught would have amused him; it was a silly, cheap little incident. But Caroline felt oddly humiliated; she was exasperated at being involved in his shabby behaviour; she was hurt that he should have shown her so little consideration. Yet at the same time, she did not want to lose the possibility of a renewal of friendship. After all, sensitive feeling was a poor companion, the time was running out, neither of them, at the most optimistic estimate, was likely to have opportunity to indulge in protracted fencing. Besides, she was unhappy and in the avoidance of that she was prepared to sacrifice a little self-pride.

'Oh, dear, I'm so tired,' said Caroline, and was startled as the telephone rang. She lifted the receiver with unsteady fingers. Her preference for being left to herself had encouraged most people to respect her liking for privacy.

'Hullo?'

'You sound very severe. Look here, can you come and lunch on Sunday, same time and place? I'll send a car to fetch you. The thing is . . .'

'You'd rather not drive over to fetch me. Mrs Bird never works for me at the week-end—and no one else does.'

'Point taken. I'll be with you at a quarter to one. Thank you, Caroline.'

'No fool like an old fool,' she told herself. To her considerable surprise the intervening interval seemed unexpectedly long. It seemed to her typical that Alex had neither apologized over the telephone nor revealed any evidence of contrition. He was, of course, impossible. Her memory of him had proved faulty, it was inevitable that the intervening years had dimmed some of the details of recollection.

It had been difficult to recall his tone of voice, its practised ease.

'Obviously I shall not mention what happened, unless he does,' said Caroline.

Chapter Eight

THE SUNLESS day was cold and damp, and driving past the dark fields she watched the storm clouds banked behind the heavy trees. If she had been young and full of the delight of anticipation, the weather might have depressed her. She remembered past excitement and the desire that sunshine and warmth should be a part of happiness; but all that was long over. What remained was only the unaccountable wish to be with him again, to hear his voice and to watch his worn face lose something of its harshness. Enthusiasm was dead and excitement perished for ever. What remained, she supposed, was the evolution of her love; devotion so long standing was very likely senseless, but it gave the only clue to her feeling. Better to admit that her life had been a waste land without him than to deny the burden of truth. And as she was rattled in a hired car towards their meeting, she deliberately put aside all feeling of resentment or contempt. She no longer harboured the hot anger she had once nourished against him. She still hated the memory of his cruelty, but she could not hate the man.

The car ground up the cinder path in front of the hotel and stopped in a series of deplorable jerks as Alex came out to meet it.

'What the blazes,' he began, as the driver opened the door which swung on a loose hinge and proceeded to fall off.

Caroline laughed while he helped her out. 'Anyhow, I got here,' she said.

'Sorry, sir,' said the driver. 'All the other cars was booked and, seeing the boss was out, not wanting to disappoint the lady, I come over in m'own.'

'Count ten, Alex!' said Caroline. 'He probably did his best.'

'The fellow's a damned fool,' he said, and led her into the hotel. 'You must have had the hell of a journey in that piece of ironmongery.'

'Rather exciting actually.'

'Most women would have been in a towering rage.'

The little panelled dining-room was, as before, half-empty. She remembered from last time the pallid young waiter with his tired half-smile.

'He had the shock of his life when I refused to order a drink while I was waiting for you,' Alex told her. 'As a matter of fact I'm on the wagon. I'll have lime juice. You prefer your meals dry, don't you, Caroline?'

'You've got a good memory, but tell me, why the abstinence?'

He grimaced. 'For the same reason that I've garaged my car. I've had another slight heart-attack. It happened at my Club a fortnight ago, and they hauled me off to hospital for a few days' rest. Which is why I didn't ring you up sooner. There's nothing to worry about; I carry some pills about with me which are supposed to do the trick if I collapse again.'

'Do they? I mean, do they give you relief?'

'Yes. I'm to go and get overhauled again in a month's time. Meantime a quiet life.'

'Have you consulted a heart specialist?'

'They sent for one when I was in the nursing home.'

'What did he say, Alex?'

'Be a good boy, no excitement, and do as you're told. And that's enough. I hate talking about my health and I'm not answering any more questions.'

'Very well.'

'Anyone else would have gone on pestering me for more details! But you're too sensitive for that. Incidentally, don't you find it's rather a handicap?'

'You mean as a curb to undue inquisitiveness?'

He laughed and she noticed how old his face had become. 'You would say that, wouldn't you? What shall we eat, something appetizing and light? You're very thin, Caroline, but it suits you. Are you well?'

'Oh, yes, on the whole.'

'What does that mean?'

'That I am. One can't resist the handicaps of one's age.'

'Such as?'

'They're quite unimportant.'

'Don't fence with me, Caroline.'

'I only meant that it's a bore to tire easily instead of being able to go for my favourite walks in the woods any more, and that, when it's cold and wet, I come to the conclusion that fresh air is a mistake.'

'So you stay at home by yourself?'

'Yes, but I don't really feel alone.'

'I don't think I believe that,' he told her.

'It's quite true. The kind of reading which I enjoy is immensely companionable.'

'It can't have taken the place of other things. When I first met you, you were still at your best. Are you telling me you ceased to live after you chucked me? It doesn't make sense, Caroline.'

The pale young waiter who brought their savoury omelets, thought them an odd pair. *She* looked his idea of a lady, very quiet and inconspicuous, and *he* looked as if he had exhausted all the pleasures of life and was burnt out. The waiter who was by way of being a student of human nature, watched them with a faint sardonic smile. That sort didn't count their change and leave a meagre tip on the plate!

Caroline was watching the raindrops slowly chasing each other down the narrow window panes. 'I'm not sure that I know what you mean by talking about *living*. One exists, one has minor enjoyments, one evolves a sort of placidity which falls slightly short of contentment and finally becomes a habit.'

'But that's all absurd,' he told her, 'apart from being a criminal waste. Look here, you once told me you had an unsatisfactory sort of love affair when you were not quite twenty. For reasons best known to yourself, you decided to wait for something which seemed, in your opinion, more worth your while. What exactly that meant I don't pretend to know. What I do know is that so far as I'm concerned, I was intrigued by you from the start because you were so damned self-contained, and then I realized that it wasn't a pose, and that annoyed me. You had no business to look so attractive and keep me at arm's length. You had a beautiful body and I wanted you; I told myself it was merely a question of time before I got you to bed. Did you know that?'

'Yes, I suppose so.'

'Of course you did, you weren't a fool. And then you went and ruined the whole thing with that bosh about being afraid you'd change your mind about your—your dislike of what you called cruelty and get to think it didn't matter. That, of course, was arrant nonsense.'

'Not to me, Alex.'

'You're basing the whole thing on my momentary spasm of irritation. Damn it all, Caroline, I didn't kill your blasted dog.'

'I don't think you would have cared if you had. When you were really furious or your pride was hurt, I don't think you would have—perhaps *could* have, controlled your anger. I'm not the only person to think that, am I?'

He gave her a quick startled glance. 'What are you talking about?'

'I know it didn't come out in the evidence during your divorce case, but you weren't exactly gentle with Milly, were you?'

'What the devil do you know about that?'

'Only that it was common knowledge you had knocked her about.'

'That for a blasted lie! I was a bit rough with her once, and once only. If you want a detailed account of what happened . . .'

'No, I don't.'

'Well, anyhow, to put the record straight, I was annoyed and I flung her against a wall with, I suppose, considerable force. Whereupon she yelled, ran out of the house and never came back. Anyhow, did you have to listen to what people said about me?'

'I was living with my brother at the time. It was he who told me. He'd heard about it at his Club. He said that the general opinion was that she'd had a lot to put up with, culminating in actual violence. I told my brother I wasn't interested.'

'Weren't you?'

'I may have used the wrong word. Anyhow, I don't listen to that kind of gossip. Apart from anything else, it never loses in the telling.'

'Most women enjoy anything that makes their idea of a good story. Presumably because they've got nothing else to talk about.'

'Some women, not "most" women, Alex.'

'If you believed that, you wouldn't go out of your way to avoid them.'

'*Touché*! But don't forget I live among a small, not very select, community.'

He was silent for a moment. 'I'm sorry,' he said slowly, 'about what happened when last I came down. But how the hell was I to know you had exchanged your daily for her pretty little fool of a daughter? I admit I'd had a drink too many . . .'

'Must we discuss it?'

'Did you mind, Caroline?'

'I thought it—it was slightly silly.'

He grimaced. 'Which about sums it up.'

She was glad that he left it at that. It seemed to her that much conversation was not necessary between them. Silence created no barrier, nor, she felt, did they need to be entertained : they could achieve an intimacy which needed no expression.

After a time, he said : 'Bored?'

'No. Of course not.'

'Happy? Oh, for Heaven's sake, don't smile at me like that, Caroline : you might just as well burst into tears.'

'Nonsense . . . anyhow, I very seldom cry. I'm too old. Only the young get relief from tears.'

'You still haven't answered my question,' he persisted. 'Put it another way, if you like : are you *un*happy, Caroline?'

'I think one outgrows even that.'

'But you were at one time? Was that because of me?'

'Does it matter now?'

'Yes, it does. It was so unlike anything else. I've made a fool of myself over a good many women. Nothing lasted longer than I wanted it to. But the fact that I couldn't make you out, put the whole thing on a different level. I wanted you for a number of reasons, probably more than I've ever wanted any woman. And I was damned certain that you loved me.'

'But you didn't love me, did you?' she said softly.

'Yes, I did, you damned fool ... I'm sorry, Caroline, but you can't say a thing like that and get away with it. You obviously thought that, because I didn't waste time with you from the start, that it was all too easy, that I took the whole thing for granted.'

'I think you did. It was going to be just another affair, wasn't it?'

'No,' he said stubbornly, 'that's where you're wrong. It wasn't. You mightn't have cared to take the risk, but I told myself, given half a chance I'd marry you and make a go of it. It wasn't as though you were a very young girl, you knew the world ...'

'I think that's a little meaningless. I knew what happened to other people, of course ...'

'Suppose it had happened to you, couldn't you have taken it? I wouldn't have bust up our marriage : I don't mind betting that you'd always have come first. If you were really fond of me, that would have been enough, wouldn't it?'

She continued to watch the raindrops chasing each other down the window panes.

'There didn't *have* to be other women,' he argued, 'there might not have been. I'm only trying to be fair.'

'I know you are.'

'Caroline, wasn't there really anyone else for you afterwards?'

'No.'

'I can hardly believe that. But I know you never tell lies. Was it because you were thinking of making it up with me some time? If so, why didn't you?'

'I couldn't. It wasn't a thing one could argue about, Alex. And, anyhow, I was right, wasn't I? When you did get

93

married, you didn't make Milly happy.'

'Milly? What the hell has she got to do with it? You were two totally different people.'

'But she loved you, presumably.'

'Well? Look here, I was fed up when I met her. I thought, I still think, you treated me abominably. You must have known I'd have done anything to get you ... *and* have made a success of it.'

'Why do you think that?'

'Because there was something about you that seemed to me unlike other women. For a start you weren't out for yourself all the time.'

'That's not unique.'

'It is in my experience. I had an odd sort of feeling that you'd impose the most absurd restrictions upon yourself, I wouldn't say exactly for moral reasons nor, I grant you, from actual cowardice, but because you had some sort of ridiculous standard which you were too obstinate to lower.'

'Or possibly too fastidious?'

He looked angry. 'Or too squeamish.'

'Are we,' she asked, 'talking about the same thing? I mean that I thought—I've always thought—cruelty the most heinous of all faults. I hate it because it's uncivilized. I think it can be the result of a kind of misguided pride quite apart from any sadistic intent ...'

'You exaggerate the whole thing,' he interrupted, his voice thick with irritation, 'a—a slight loss of temper isn't evidence of a constant mood and no one but a fool would think it was. After all, there's nothing particularly praiseworthy in the avoidance of any kind of conflict.'

'Did I suggest that there was? But there can't be any genuine meeting place when there's a chasm between values. At least, I think not ... I don't suppose you'll understand, but the whole thing has been a perpetual sorrow for me.'

'But that was entirely your own fault, Caroline,' he interrupted. 'Surely you could have given the thing a chance.'

The young waiter watched them without expression. He had long ago overcome surprise at the spectacle of neglected food. Waste he had grown used to. In his home there was never quite enough to eat. Life was composed of inequality. Funny the way these two just didn't seem interested in a square meal.

'Tired, Caroline?'

'No.'

'You sighed as if you were.'

'I didn't know I had.'

'It's a curse not having my car. Can't we go and sit outside?'

'It's still raining.'

'Oh, hell!'

'There's a lounge of sorts.'

'I know there is, I passed it on the way in. There are three old trouts, knitting revolting garments, in the only available armchairs.'

'I find it awfully hard to realize that I'm an old trout myself.'

'You're not. You're the wrong shape. You don't *feel* old, do you?'

'Sometimes.'

'You're not half as independent as you pretend to be,' he told her.

'I've been on my own for a good many years. I don't need people very much, you know.'

'That for a tale. You know as well as I do that you're horribly thin-skinned.'

'Perhaps that's partly the reason why I like to avoid being at risk.'

'What's that supposed to mean?' he demanded.

'That I prefer not to be at the mercy of other people's moods. I'm too old, Alex.'

'For what?'

'For instability. I want peace and quiet.'

'Fair enough. So do I.'

She smiled at him. 'Since when? Isn't it just because you're not very well?'

'No, of course it isn't. You don't believe me, do you? All right, if you really want to know, I do feel rotten ... I thought that would shake you a bit ... Caroline, be sensible. I'm not asking for anything, but surely there's no ostensible reason why we shouldn't be friends. It's what we both want.'

'Yes ... But could I make things any better for you? I can't see how that's possible.'

'You underrate yourself, don't you?' he said sarcastically. 'What about the other side of it. Do I do anything for you? Come along, tell me.'

'I have told you.'

'Tell me again.'

'I don't think we mean the same thing by friendship, Alex.'

'You've got love and loyalty inextricably linked, haven't you?' he said.

'If it's the real thing, it has to be.'

'And you can say that still?'

'Yes.'

'But,' he persisted, 'it hasn't made you happy, has it? I can't imagine what you got out of it all ... You're not telling me you didn't want anything else? You had plenty to offer, you were still young, you were attractive, intelligent, responsive, and other things perhaps we'd better not enumerate. And more or less deliberately you let the whole thing slide. I suppose you blame me.'

'No. It was my own choice.'

He looked at her for a long moment without speaking. 'You couldn't have given me more convincing proof of your feeling for me. There's one thing certain, I've never felt like this about any other woman. At least you believe that, don't you?'

'Yes, I think I do.'

'Well, doesn't that mean anything to you?'

'Of course it does. But the point is, isn't it, Alex, whatever you say, that the chances are you'd have got just as tired of me as you did of all the others.'

'No, I wouldn't.'

'Apart from which, I couldn't ever have overcome my fear, Alex—though it went much deeper than that—that fundamentally you weren't kind. It may sound trite or anything else you like to call it, but nothing can take its place however much one may try to hoodwink oneself into believing that it's not all-important. Now that I'm old I can see much more clearly, but I think I knew, even then, that although I loved you, I was hiding the truth from myself. I think that was probably what made me so desperately unhappy.'

His fingers were unsteady as he fumbled with his cigarette case. 'It seems to me you created your own difficulties. Shall we go and sit outside?'

'It's still raining.' But she was doubtful if he heard her : his eyes were fixed, not on her but on the opposite wall.

'You never answered my letter,' he said.

'It's all a long time ago, Alex.'

His breath was laboured as the thick dark colour faded from his face. 'I'm not sure that those damned tablets they've given me don't have some sort of side-effects,' he said. 'When I see my doctor again I'll tell him to change them. I'm really all right, you know, except that now and then I more or less lose track of where I am, and I get a sort of falling sensation

97

as though I were tight.'

'Don't you think it would be a good idea if you rang up your doctor and asked him to see you tomorrow?'

'Not if it means going back to the nursing home.'

'Mightn't that be the quickest way of getting well again? You're not being looked after in your flat, are you? And I think that's what you need. After all, in hospital they've got nurses about during the night, and if you want something to help you sleep, there they are.'

'Something in that. Would you come and visit me?'

'Of course, if you want me to.'

'It's absurd, you know, I got quite frightened one night—it was early morning actually, and I thought I was really for it. I didn't know what a stiff drink would do to me and I funked risking it.'

'Ring up your doctor when you get back and tell him to book you a bed for tomorrow. He'll come along in the morning and arrange everything. Paying patients don't have to wait in a queue.'

He rubbed his forehead fretfully. 'Oh, I don't know. I might feel better tomorrow.'

'May I come back with you and do all the donkey work? I won't fuss you, I promise, but I could help you to get your things together.'

'All right,' he said wearily, and taking out his pocket book, signalled to the waiter. 'You do that. You can ring up the chap from my flat.'

'I expect the people at the desk here can get hold of a car for us,' she said, and wondered whether she dared put a hand below his elbow as they moved towards the hall.

To her surprise he walked steadily and spoke clearly to the receptionist, who was young and pretty and afforded him smile for smile.

When he joined Caroline beside the window, he sat down

and laughed. 'Incredibly efficient, aren't they?' he said. 'She says a car will be round in five minutes. I expect they'll charge the earth, but never mind, I don't see you every day of the week.'

'What news of your boy?' she asked presently, as they drove across the wet lanes towards London.

'None,' he said, a little pettishly. 'Why should there be?'

'No reason.'

'Sandy's Milly's business,' he said. 'I'm afraid he doesn't interest me in the very least bit in this world. I see him, as I told you, at long intervals which bores us both quite incredibly. His idea of violent dissipation is to fish with Tom Garland in Scotland.'

'Does Milly go with them?'

'I suppose so. Damp tweed and persistent fog is probably her idea of a superb holiday.' His mouth took an ugly twist as he added: 'Why on earth I ever married her, I'm damned if I know. Half the time her unspeakable foolishness drove me round the bend.'

'Don't run her down, Alex.'

'That's all very well. You don't know what it was like living with her . . . Oh, of course, she was all sweetness and light . . . she agreed with everything I said, though I knew dam' well she hated half of it and merely wanted to keep the peace. It was her idea of being a virtuous wife.'

'How old was Sandy when she left you?'

'Two or three, I forget exactly . . . You'd have thought, from what that fellow said, I was beyond the pale . . . blasted fool, what's his name . . .'

'Tom Garland?'

'No, that's not right, is it? . . . Perhaps it is.'

'Driving always makes me sleepy at this time of day,' she said. 'Don't let's bother to talk.'

'All right.' He was frowning and rubbed his eyes, blinking.

She wished that their journey was over. Her simulated fatigue might, she hoped, induce him to keep quiet. It was with relief that she saw his head nod and his hands lie inert on his knees. If only he could sleep until she got him to his flat and within reach of a telephone!

Time dragged, but he lolled against her, and she put a supporting arm round him. His deep colour had returned and his breathing seemed to her very heavy.

The afternoon darkened and rain fell and danced upon the roads. The country lay behind them; great blocks of buildings flanked the wet pavements. At last the car drew up beside the faceless flats with their flower beds and their air of smug affluence.

'Alex,' she said quietly.

A little to her surprise, he woke easily and sat up, squaring his shoulders. 'I appear to have dropped off,' he said. 'That stuff my doctor gives me has a soporific effect. Come along, my flat's on the ground floor.'

The room into which he led her seemed stale and airless. Petulantly he opened the windows: sheets of the morning's newspaper flapped in the wet wind. The leather armchairs were arranged in prim precision round a small table bearing an empty glass ash tray.

'They send in an old hag for an hour each morning,' Alex said. 'She makes my bed, cleans the bath and, I've a shrewd suspicion, drinks my whisky. Sit down, Caroline ... Forty years ago if you hadn't been so incredibly obstinate ...'

'Don't you think it's a little pointless to go over old ground? I'd rather not spoil our friendship with argument. Can't we just enjoy it for what it is?'

'I suppose so. But that doesn't prevent me from cursing the indisputable fact that I didn't know how to deal with you. It would have been better for both of us if I had. I let you go because ...'

'You had no option.'

'I wouldn't say that. I could have contrived a meeting, I could have forced you . . .'

'But you didn't, and that at least was wise.'

'I'm not so sure. One thing I *am* certain of is that being what you are, you can't have persuaded yourself that the life you chose was the right one. You're not going to pretend you were happy, are you?'

'We've been into that before, haven't we? *Please*, Alex.'

'All right. It doesn't make sense to me, but let it go. If you loathed the sight of me, why did you let me come back? Incidentally, it's damned stuffy in here, we'd better have another window open.'

'They *are* both open, Alex . . .' and added as he fumbled with his jacket buttons : 'May I do that for you?' Her fingers touched the inside pocket and drew out a little phial.

'Two,' he said.

She shook them into her palm and gave them to him. 'Here you are, darling.'

After he had swallowed the tablets, she loosened his tie and his collar, and sat down quietly until his strangled breath became quiet.

'May I ring your doctor now?'

'You may not . . . he'll be on his rounds; if you like to stay until five you can catch him at the surgery. But I'll be all right.'

'Very well.'

'You didn't panic . . . d'you know what you called me?'

'Instead of asking questions, I think it would be very sensible if you went to bed. You can manage, can't you? Meanwhile I'll fill a hot water bottle. Is there one in your bathroom? Don't hurry to get up, take your time.'

'Where did you learn all this?'

'I didn't. It's just commonsense.'

He raised himself to his feet and pulled off his dangling tie with distaste. 'Will you come and sit beside me? I've got some brandy in my room. I'm allowed a tot, if we count this as an emergency.'

'Why not? Call me when you're ready.'

Presently she sat down to wait, aware that she was very tired. She hoped the doctor would insist on sending him back to the nursing home. She was sure that it was unsafe to leave him alone. Yet when she saw him sitting up in his bed, she thought that he looked surprisingly recovered.

'Bit of a fraud, aren't I?' he said.

'I'm glad to see you've got a telephone beside you,' she said. 'You will ring up your doctor this evening, won't you?'

'I suppose so ... all right, I will. I'm nearly out of these blasted tablets anyhow. Pity you don't live nearer, Caroline. Don't you get sick to death of village life?'

'Probably I would if I belonged to it : luckily I don't. I just love the quiet, and the beauty of it all.'

'It occurs to me as being pretty ordinary country.'

'It is. Everything on a small scale, little woods and ponds, flowers in tiny cottage gardens, old-fashioned farms; I think it's rather engaging.'

'You ran away with a vengeance, didn't you, Caroline?'

'If you choose to look at it like that. Is there more reality in cities, and noise?'

'Probably.'

'Most town-dwellers only occupy a small corner of it. And aren't their friends all much of a muchness?'

'What are you trying to prove, Caroline?'

'I'm not trying to *prove* anything. I simply think that a variety of people is more apparent than real. If their interests are sufficiently intelligent and their opportunities are adequate, then, of course, they're in luck's way. But, as a general rule, I think the majority simply enjoy the mixture as before : especially if they happen to be hedonists.'

'You're not in the kindest of moods, are you?' he returned. 'If the truth were known, you've got a pretty poor opinion of me, haven't you?'

'No.'

'Put another way, you don't much like me, even if you love me, do you, Caroline?'

'Alex, you're tired. Settle down and have a sleep. I'm going home now. When you've seen the doctor, ring me up and tell me what your plans are.'

'Can't you stay a bit longer?'

'I'll come again. May I have the number of your garage?'

'I'll do it. Tell them to put the car down to me ... Come again soon, Caroline.'

'Of course I will.' She stood watching him, while he took up the telephone. She hoped that her voice was sufficiently matter-of-fact. The pain in her heart seemed stifling. 'You'll order your dinner to be sent up to you, won't you?'

'Oddly enough,' he said with a return to his customary off-hand irony, 'that is one of the functions of a service flat.'

She was aware of an odd sense of gratitude : had he been gentle, she doubted if she would have been able to bear it.

Chapter Nine

'I DO so dislike railway stations,' said Milly tearfully. 'I always want to cry when the train goes off.'

'Sweetheart, you would dislike it still more if it remained sympathetically immobile,' declared Tom Garland, 'and thus postponed the relief ... I mean, the distress ... of carting our loved ones out of sight for a few weeks. Incidentally, I did suggest taking Sandy by road, you remember.'

'Yes dear, but I thought the other boys would notice if they happened to be about. I mean, he'd be the only one coming back at half-term and they might tease him.'

'Darling, they're public school men, not private school brats.'

'Oh, I know, Tom. I thought last Speech Day how sophisticated some of them looked. Two or three had dreadful side-whiskers.'

'It's not *necessarily* a sign of extreme depravity, you know. Come along, we will now go and drink some horrible railway tea and consume a couple of equally revolting buns. After which, we will take a taxi to Waterloo, and catch our train back to rural civilization.'

'I do hope Sandy remembered to put away that crossword puzzle he was trying to solve before he left. He'd filled in several spaces, and I can't help thinking it looks rather sad.'

'Leave it to me and I'll hide it, directly we get home, while you trot off to the loo and have a good cry, followed by a couple of aspirins and then come down and we'll listen-in to a who-dun-it, which I may remark in parenthesis, enchants all gentle little sweetie-pies like you with an insatiable love for blood and thunder. Don't ask me why, ask the BBC, they understand human nature.'

Milly dried her eyes gratefully. 'Of course the plays never seem actually *real* to me. They're always about such horrid people.'

'Which, villains or victims? In the interests of morality, both have to be presented as extremely undesirable. That makes everybody happy. It gives most of us an enormous sense of satisfaction to reflect upon the wickedness and perfidy of the rest.'

'Some people,' said Milly sadly, 'think I was wicked when I ran away from Alex. They said it was bad enough leaving him, but worse that I involved you as well.'

'So you have told me more than once, darling. The fact that you have made me superlatively happy, provided Sandy with a congenial home, and rescued yourself from a disastrous situation, may not have occurred to your rather less than amiable critics as an eminently sensible thing to have done, but that's neither here nor there. Alex was and probably still is a cad. I doubt if there was any woman in his life, and from what one hears there were plenty of them, who wouldn't agree with that as a fair summing up. No blame could conceivably attach itself to you. He bullied you into marrying him and then treated you abominably. And that's all there is to it.'

'*You* didn't ever think it was wicked of me to have stopped loving him when he behaved so badly, did you, Tom?'

'I'd have thought you singularly lacking in commonsense if you had done anything else, my pet.'

'Oh dearest, you do say the sweetest things!' declared Milly, clasping his arm as they walked away in a manner which greatly impeded their progress down the platform, but did nothing to decrease his amiability. Her distress at parting with Sandy for the length of a shortened school term had already begun to lessen. Provided with a pair of steel-rimmed spectacles, and a medical certificate for his housemaster, he had returned in his customary mood of gloomy resignation. What would happen next she was content to leave to God and dear Tom. It seemed to her that the past was an unhappy episode which was better forgotten. Of course she owed darling Sandy to Alex but she was unable to feel any gratitude to him. He had been so irritable during her pregnancy, so bored when the baby arrived. She had no surviving parents to advise her, and her worldly-wise friends had provided her with information which startled her a good deal. Men, they assured her, were like that, possessing, almost invariably, unbridled passions and unfortunate tastes. Which gratuitous piece of information made poor Milly extremely unhappy.

She was all the more thankful to discover that quite the converse was true of dear Tom. He was both manly and kind, he never used foul language in the presence of women, he did not think people who got drunk were in the least funny, and, until he had nearly reached middle age, had always taken a great deal of exercise which his venerable mother had declared was an excellent substitute for other less commendable forms of amusement.

When she died he was almost immediately consoled by the unexpected advent of Milly, who delighted him by being just the sort of sweet-tempered little silly he considered most companionable. He went through the divorce court with calm : its requirements seemed to him much less formidable than he had expected : he had never liked riverside hotels but adultery in such charming surroundings seemed a small price to pay for a prejudice not put to the test before. With considerable rapidity he and Milly were married without undue excitement. He continued to play golf, gave up breeding polo ponies, put on weight, and was delighted to discover that married life was so pleasant.

When they reached home, he mixed himself a drink, placed Sandy's unfinished crossword puzzle in the waste-paper basket, and walked round the garden a couple of times, refreshed by a cool breeze and the sight of late-afternoon sunshine on the wet roses.

The prevailing discord beyond the enclosure of his own small world failed to disturb him. He had fought with a victorious army and welcomed peace as a respite, not an answer. While politicians wrangled, arms piled up, and idealists closed their minds to unpalatable facts, he remained unshaken in his belief that until calamity overtook its victims, it was wise to ignore its possibility. Not only with words but in his manner of living he protected those dependent upon him with his easy-going philosophy. His affectionate nature was wholly satisfied by his warm relationship with his wife, and without taking it all too seriously, he liked being a stepfather. He helped Milly to choose Sandy's schools carefully, and was relieved that Alex took no interest in his selection beyond paying the bills each term by a banker's order and commenting once or twice, with some acidity, on the boy's continued delicacy. But since, fortunately, his remarks were addressed by letter to Sandy's housemaster who was used to the unreason of most parents, especially those who had delegated their responsibility to others, the matter ended there.

'I suppose,' said Milly tentatively at supper that evening, 'we ought to be thinking about what Sandy is going to be, eventually.'

'All in good time,' Tom assured her comfortably. 'Ruling out the Services, the Church, the learned professions, commerce, the stage, and the arts, the choice is presumably wide.'

'I wondered about banking, only he's not very good at figures. But I think someone told me that doesn't matter nowadays. They do everything by machine—I don't quite understand how, but it can't make mistakes. It doesn't actually work by itself, does it, Tom? Like a robot?'

'No, darling: the human element is retained in order to make possible some degree of error.'

'Oh dear! I don't think Sandy would quite understand all that ... I wonder whether he'd like farming. It would be nice for him to be in the open air all the time, and, of course, they don't have much to do with bulls nowadays because of AI. I wonder sometimes if the cows mind: I mean it's so impersonal.'

'Judging by what I've seen, I should think some of them prefer it ... Well, after all that, shall we decide against Cambridge and send Sandy to an agricultural college? I don't suppose his father would have any strong feeling about it one way or the other.'

'I remember,' said Milly, 'what Alex used to say about girls on the land and— and that kind of thing. Of course he always imagined sex was, as it were, in everything, if you know what I mean. I don't think Sandy will turn out like that, do you?'

'Not for a moment.'

'You *are* such a comfort to me, Tom.'

'Isn't that what I'm here for?'

He had wandered off by himself to lie in the sun on the river bank. It was a relief to escape from other members of his house, from blatant hilarity, noisy good nature and cheerful smut. He was bored by jokes he didn't entirely understand, by the magazines a chap in his study had concealed from authority between the pages of the *National Geographic Magazine*; confused by memory of the girl, Elizabeth, his father had made him take to the cinema. Sandy didn't want to think about her, nor to listen to the ribald stories the Captain of Boats thought so amusing, nor to look again at the photographs in the forbidden magazines over which the other two occupants of his study pored and giggled.

He wanted to get away from it all, to hear his mother's gentle platitudes and his stepfather's jolly amiability. He was safe there, he could swallow his tonic and consent to going to bed early, and be pleased when he climbed on the bathroom scales to find that he was still underweight.

The warm sun stroked his face; he took off his spectacles and rubbed his hot eyes. Gnats droned above the quiet river, on the other side beyond the rushes a flotilla of little ducks swam in their mother's wake, a dragon fly flashed brilliant blue in audacious competition against the cloudless sky. From the small thatched farm beyond the sentinel poplars came the intermittent lowing of golden cows.

The boy sat up and hugged his knees; somewhere a church bell softened by distance was summoning a straggle of villagers to Vespers. It was time that he went back to school. There was no chapel this evening, only a few minutes of rapid House prayers before lock-up. The new, young, and energetic headmaster was trying to instil in six hundred boys a sense of the value of Divine worship on Sunday by curtailing its practice to a brief Morning Service and voluntary attendance at a celebration of the Holy Eucharest in the evening once a month. The older masters who had seen these efforts before smiled and sighed. They understood boys better than any new broom who had yet to taste the sour fruit of disillusion.

Sandy had often listened to his friends' sometimes ribald

comments on the Services in chapel : when he was younger he had been upset at the thought that God might be offended : now he had come to the reluctant conclusion that in all probability God was more broad-minded than he expected. Perhaps it didn't really matter what anybody thought. It gave him more of a sense of insecurity than liberation; he didn't quite like it. At his private school he had, from the age of nine until he was thirteen, been confined by rules which could only be breached at risk. Punishment in his view made sense. He had heard people, who went to more modern establishments, say that it was terribly old-fashioned to believe in sin. He did not like to ask his mother what she thought or to request Tom's opinion. He felt sure that they would be surprised that he should concern himself with such matters. He had been prepared for Confirmation by his present headmaster's predecessor who, on the brink of retirement, had been at pains wearily to assure the candidates sent to him for religious instruction that such sins of the flesh to which they might be tempted to succumb in adolesence would inevitably lead to severe mental disorder or raving lunacy. The more sophisticated of his victims received his comments with calm. 'My father's a doctor,' said one of them, 'he says that's bunkum.'

Sandy was relieved to hear it. Sitting on the river bank he watched the waters grow cool and dark. He thought of Elizabeth and her pretty, unkind smile. He did not want to remember her, she had teased him and made him feel stupid : his father had thought him a fool. But Alex had been a beast to his mother so probably all his conclusions were wrong. He was sure that Tom thought so. His stepfather was a kind man : all the same it was impossible to tell him about those magazines which the fellows in his study had concealed among the pages of the respectable *National Geographic*; he hadn't wanted to see them but he couldn't forget them. He couldn't forget Elizabeth either.

Slowly he pulled himself up and brushed the loose grass from his Sunday suit. The ducklings had left the river and were sheltering from the gathering evening chill against their mother.

He had a sudden absurd desire to cry. He wondered whether other fellows ever felt like that, but it seemed extremely unlikely. Most of them regarded him with a mild amusement; he offended nobody, he did his work in a steady unspectacular fashion, and his lack of success at games was accepted quite agreeably as due to nothing more heinous than physical delicacy. He was not made to feel a freak or a shirker : he was merely ignored in a tolerant fashion. In a sense, he was a product of their society : he accepted his lowly place without resentment, maintaining a shyness which was not unhappy. It was only lately that he had become conscious of a restlessness that he could not under-stand. Now and again he was irritated by his mother's ab-sorption in him, and at the same time offended if it seemed that she was paying more attention to Tom than to himself. He was ashamed of these sensations : he longed for Milly's uncritical affection when he was away from her, and when, at home, he was ill he felt that there was no one in the world like her. He found it all very upsetting. He tried to sort it out by himself; he had an idea that when he was alone he could think more clearly. The noise and activity of a wholly masculine society deprived him of the ability to steady his mind. His imagination was disturbed by day dreams which he felt sure were wrong; sometimes he tried to make them into a coherent whole with a beginning, a middle, and an end. But that was too difficult. He could lie in the sun beside the river and make some attempt to think of beauty without knowing what he meant by it.

'Other people,' he muttered, 'don't seem to get in such

a muddle as I do. Half the time everything seems so senseless ... and then it clears up for some reason.' But nothing
seemed to last. What was the word? *Mutability*. He knew
some lines about that,

> 'All that we wish to stay
> Tempts and then flies ...
> ... Virtue how frail it is!
> Friendship how rare!'

Poets, in his opinion, were seldom happy people. Perhaps
in another year or two he would ease his sense of troubled
perplexity by writing verse himself. It might help.

He began to walk back towards the House: tea was at
six, he would open the jar of shrimp paste which Milly had
sent him and spread it on a thick slice of bread and butter.
One of the fellows in his study had been sent a large tin of
Devonshire cream, the other chap was in training for the
Hundred. 'You can have my share,' he told Sandy, though
strictly speaking it wasn't his to offer. But the owner,
heaping a scone with blackberry jam on top of the cream,
had grinned and said: 'Help yourself, it won't keep. I caught
my fag licking the tin clean once. Fat lot of satisfaction he
got out of that!'

'If it wasn't for our people at home,' said the sprinter,
'we'd die of starvation.'

'I trust when I leave here I shall never eat cow again.'

'Do we?'

'Well I never came across good honest beef which tasted
like the muck we're offered.'

'It's probably old horse.'

Sandy, who had heard it all before, wished that he dared
join in, but he didn't know what to say lest his opinion be
regarded as superfluous. He had frequently found it possible
surreptitiously to supply his immediate neighbour in hall
with a slice or two off his own luncheon plate. He was sel-

dom hungry, but he knew that the criticisms launched against school food were not intended to be taken seriously. The swells had to boast of superior knowledge of what was palatable.

Strolling along the towpath, he watched a little moorhen swim across the smooth water : he wished that he had an equal sense of direction and happy certainty. Everything was very still, soon he would be back among the clamour and the sound of thudding feet. Sunday was nearly over. The Sabbatical quiet was not like the abrupt silence hanging over an urban Sunday. There it seemed as if a temporary cessation of noise was heavily reluctant. In rural places peace seemed to rest upon the hills, to linger in the damp woods, to pause in the twisting lanes. Nothing was hurried or confusing. What was it the girl Elizabeth had said : *'Don't you want to grow up? ... I'm younger than you are, but I wouldn't mind betting I know more, it's about time you woke up ...'*

Although he sometimes found Tom's incessant heartiness trying, he rather envied his stepfather's capacity for enjoyment. It was never forced. He appreciated his food with the gusto of a schoolboy but without his greed, he laughed at other people's jokes and at his own, and above all, he was kind. Sandy knew that Tom helped to create harmony in the home and that his mother basked in a simple contentment.

'It's not their fault,' he told himself, 'it's mine ... at least I suppose so ... I used to like fishing with Tom—well, I do still but I can't whack up an awful lot of enthusiasm about it, and poor Mummy's idea of arranging a treat for the three of us, going off to a point-to-point or a polo match, which they both adore, bores me stiff, though I have to pretend that it doesn't. I don't really want to do things *with* them always ... or with anybody ... it's so *boring* ...'

A small cheerful fag made their tea in the study. He was

an efficient little boy and refrained from either breaking their china or helping himself to the clotted cream. Sandy wished that he had as much self-command. His face was burnt pink from the sun and his head ached a little. When their fag left them, the others turned on the gramophone and opening the *National Geographic* again, sought its less instructive enclosure.

'I like the one with the bracelet or whatever, round her ankle . . .'

'I like the red-haired one with the poppy between her teeth . . .'

Sandy hoped they wouldn't ask him which one he liked best : the dark-haired girl reminded him of Elizabeth : he wondered whether she too would look like that with nothing on . . .

He took out a book from his shelf and began to read. He felt sleepy after the long afternoon in the sun; lying back in the basket chair, he read on. His head began to loll, he blinked and his eyelids fell; not until the bell for House prayers sounded was he recalled from his dreams.

Chapter Ten

'I'M HIDEOUSLY bored,' complained Alex. He pushed aside
the crumpled newspapers lying on the neatly folded counter-
pane. Everything in the nursing home bedroom had the
impersonal character proper to frequent changes of tenancy.
The pale immaculate walls, the brilliantly polished floor, the
two deep armchairs bearing no evidence of ever having been
sat upon, the shrill green silk screen, the clean books in the
small shelf, all gave him a sense of lost identity. He had
always retained a soldier's neatness, but it had been a tidiness
of his own selection. Even his shaving brushes and sponges
on the shelf above the wide basin looked too well shaken and
squeezed to be familiar.

Beyond the windows was a trim urban square. Expensive
cars made noiseless arrivals and departures. There were no
raised voices.

'I'm damned if I could stand much more of this,' he told
Caroline.

'You're looking much better.'

'Exactly. There was no reason why I shouldn't have gone
back to my flat last week.'

'I think there was every reason. You needed care and a
complete rest. Also, for once in a way, you've had to do as
you're told.'

He made a face. 'They're certainly efficient. One can
endure that sort of thing when one's powers of resistance are

limited, but so far as I'm concerned the briefer that period is, the better. By the way, I've had an unexpected visitor.'

'A welcome one?'

'It would, I suppose, be ungracious to call it anything else. She caught me unawares sitting in the sunshine on the bench outside to which the entire nursing staff had escorted me.'

'So many?'

'To be exact, two. But corpulent women in starched aprons occur to me as constituting a crowd. Elizabeth optimistically wearing an exiguous sunsuit occupied less space.'

'Which,' asked Caroline, 'of your many admirers is Elizabeth?'

'Her people live in the flats beyond mine where, one gathers, she occasionally visits them. This charitable act, I fancy, takes place when she wants something out of them. She's a complete little bitch.'

'Alluring?'

'Naturally. By the way, there's talk of moving me to a convalescent home by the sea, which would be one degree worse than this is.'

'Why not go, just for a short time?'

'It would be unmitigated hell.'

'You can't tell until you've tried, now can you? If the weather's kind you could engage a room with a balcony and sit out of doors all day long, acquiring a splendid tan.'

'Visited by the other convalescents no doubt, affluent old women with blue hair and scarlet finger nails, or ex-colonels with liver complaints and a boring collection of stale and very dirty stories. That's not a very brilliant suggestion, Caroline. Incidentally, I like your hat.'

'More women of my age ought to wear hats. It helps.'

He chuckled and looked less sour. 'D'you know I had an idea in the night. If instead of a convalescent home I went down to some spa, would you come as my guest? No strings attached, nurse companion or, more likely, an old friend met by chance. Say "yes", Caroline, you'd amuse me.'

'I'd rather say "no", Alex. I'm too old to be an amusing companion. Actually I don't think I ever was with you.'

'With other people?'

'Who didn't matter. You've never quite realized, Alex, I was in love with you to such a crippling extent that it rendered me silent and stupid. It sounds idiotic but it's true. In a sense you took everything I'd got.'

'Except one thing.'

'Yes. But, I repeat, it's all a very long time ago.'

'And you'd rather forget it ... go on, say something, you would, wouldn't you?'

'No.'

'Why not?'

'I couldn't, even if I wanted to.'

'Did you want to?'

'I suppose I did. It's possible to cling even to unhappiness if it's the only reality left.'

'That seems to me completely unreasonable.' He looked impatient. 'Why on earth torture yourself? I could say why on earth did you make so much of the whole affair but I might just as well ask myself why so inconclusive a thing has remained in my own mind all these years.'

'I'm sorry if it's worried you.'

'What the hell do you want to say it like that for? It's not characteristic of you to be bitter.'

'I don't think I'm bitter, I certainly didn't mean to give that impression. All that I said—or rather meant to say— was that you don't have to pretend with me, Alex. That's why it seems a little unrealistic to make out that it ever had any real importance to you. I accepted that long ago.'

'And didn't mind?' She was silent beneath the sting of

his impatience. 'Well, did you?'

'I didn't expect you to alter just because I loved you.'

'You had an odd way of showing you loved me ... all right, don't look like that : I never doubted it. That's what made the whole thing so baffling. I knew perfectly well you were disastrously truthful. I could have dealt with you more easily if you hadn't hung on to your beastly honesty at my expense.'

'That's one way of looking at it! I'm sorry, Alex.'

'And so you dam' well ought to be,' he snapped. 'Good heavens, Caroline, you infuriated me and broke your own heart ... And what possible good did it do you? You had to have it all your own way, of course. That goes without saying.'

'Don't you think it would be as well if we talked of something else?'

'Tell me just this, what did you get out of the whole thing?'

'You've asked me that before, more than once.'

'I may have, but you've never given me a satisfactory answer. It still doesn't make sense.'

'Does it have to?'

'Of course it does. Well, anyhow, tell me again. There can't be any harm in that. Don't you like admitting it?'

'Not very much.'

'That's cowardly. Do you wish the whole thing had never happened?'

'No.'

'Well then, why not?'

'Because,' she said slowly, 'one can't just dismiss something because it causes one sorrow ... I lived with it for so long it became, as it were, a familiar pain, a strange sort of companion which other people would probably think quite absurd, or even laughable. But that wasn't the way I looked at it . . . I can't give you a more rational explanation, Alex.'

His tired eyes explored her face with their oddly penetrating gaze. 'It mattered as much as all that? Why did you let it? Well, I suppose you couldn't help yourself. I can't imagine your ever vulgarizing a love affair into a sort of set pattern with each step enjoyably familiar, going in deeper, becoming slightly querulous and then finally cooling off. You're not like that, Caroline. Your obvious retort might be that I am. That's as it may be, but there are always exceptions to every rule. I don't know what might have happened, anything—or nothing. I could have killed you when you gave me the bird . . . I couldn't believe that you meant it. I always felt that somehow or other you'd come back. I told myself I wouldn't give you exactly a friendly reception if you did, but I knew dam' well that I would, given half a chance. Several girls I came across subsequently said it was obvious I hated women : they said I was a cynic and a pretty sour one. Of course I can't put all that down to you, I was never a sentimentalist. But the fact of the matter is that I wasn't able to forget you : you were a peculiar sort of obsession. I can sum up most women without too much difficulty. They generally fall into some known category, but you never did. I used to go over the whole thing from time to time, but I never came to any clear conclusion. It wasn't as if you had any absurd moral scruples against having an affair with me, or that in spite of your refusal to commit yourself you were fundamentally unresponsive. I knew dam' well when I held you in my arms there was no nonsense of that sort. I was morally certain that I could have talked you round. *Caroline*, you're not feeling rotten, are you?'

'No, of course not.'

'You looked as if you were going to faint.'

'I never faint. But I'd rather we didn't go on. And you're

looking tired, Alex. I must go back.'

'No, not yet. Do you prefer a spa or the sea?'

'The sea every time.'

'Then we'll settle on that.'

'I'll come down for the day, Alex.'

'What, to the West Country? Don't be absurd. Good heavens, what earthly objection could there be to staying at the same hotel at our time of life? Apart from anything else I'm ill, aren't I?'

'I should get on your nerves, Alex.'

'No, you wouldn't,' he interrupted irritably. 'That's just an excuse. What's your real reason?'

'I don't want to spoil what I've got,' she explained, 'and if we saw each other every day, that's what inevitably would happen. You might feel tired and out of humour, and perhaps the other people in the hotel would bore you and make you cross.'

'Why the blazes should they matter? I'm inviting you to come for the obvious reason that I should enjoy having you to myself.'

'You can tell me all about it when you come back.'

'Oh hell! I shan't go at all if you're going to be so damned obstinate. Are you trying to make out that it would be too great a strain for you? Forgive me for saying it, but I should have thought, judging by what you say of your feeling for me still, that you'd quite welcome seeing a good deal of me for a week or two.'

She said nothing : if he had no objection to tedious repetition, she had. He had become an exhausting companion : it seemed as though there was nothing fresh to talk about, no new triviality on which they could find common ground.

'What became of that spaniel you used to have?'

'He died at a ripe old age.'

'It's an incredible thing,' he asserted, 'that you could

break off everything just for the sake of—what happened.'

'It was a symptom, wasn't it? Alex, we've worn all that thin. There's no possible point in going over the old ground again and again. Suppose we're agreed that I *have* made myself unnecessarily and constantly sad, that was the way it happened.'

'It was incredibly stupid.'

'So are a great many loyalties.'

'To whom,' he protested, 'are you trying to make out that you were loyal? Obviously not to me.'

'You don't think to both of us? To you because you've mattered more than anything else in all my life . . .'

'And?'

'To myself for what I chose to consider was more important than a denial of honesty.'

'I don't understand what you mean,' he said petulantly.

'Lies told to oneself are the most damaging lies, I think. I had to see you as, at least, you seemed to me. And what I saw I loved, however irrational that might have appeared to be. But there had to be a reservation which I couldn't ignore. You would have known that I kept back an admiration you couldn't do without, and you'd have hated me for it. And I should have despised myself.'

'You're talking absolute arrant rubbish!'

'Don't be angry,' she said gently. 'I told you, didn't I, that I'd rather we dropped the whole subject. You see, I think I don't look at love in quite such a simple, or if you prefer it, uncomplicated way as you do. For me it was not just a hunger, it contained so much else.'

'Such as?'

'Pride, I suppose, among other things. I don't think I realized that exactly at the time though I do now. I was too angry and too miserable. But—I don't suppose you'll understand this or think that it could conceivably have seemed important, but I wanted to believe that quite apart from any attraction, I had to be convinced that you were kind, that you were incapable of any sort of cruelty, that your mind was considerate.'

'Well, I suppose that was as true of me as of most men. Why make such a thing about it? I can't believe you'd ever have got fond of anyone completely lacking in spirit.'

'No, I wouldn't. But we were talking, or I was, of self-control. Perhaps there's not very much value set on that nowadays. But it's an essential part of sane living, isn't it?'

'If we're going to argue, there's not very much point in your staying on, is there?'

'No,' said Caroline, and got up.

'You always get the better of me,' he complained, and held her hand in his unsteady fingers. 'You're partly right and more than a little wrong, but I'm not going into all that now. I agree it's better dropped. Look here, if I make some arrangement about staying in one of the less ghastly south coast hotels, you will change your mind about joining me, won't you? I don't need nursing but—but it's damned boring on one's own.'

'I'll come,' said Caroline.

Chapter Eleven

'Well, all I can say,' declared Mr Bird, 'it don't seem right to me. You can't pick up a daily paper without it's full of sex this, sex that, and not even straightforward as you might say.'

'Yes, well you needn't go on about it,' returned his wife. 'I suppose there must be some who like reading it, else it wouldn't get printed. I don't mind telling you there was a bit which came with the groceries last week which I tore up and put on the stove.'

'Best place for it,' said her husband, 'pity more hasn't got your sense. At one time people wouldn't have dared speak open about some things, let alone write about them. I wouldn't call myself narrow-minded, not after over twenty years in the Navy, but no matter whether it's the papers or the telly, there's enough in both to make you wonder where it'll stop. You can't be surprised some of the young 'uns go wrong these days when it's thrust under their noses all the time.'

Mrs Bird sniffed. 'If you ask me I reckon the older ones are as bad, if not worse. Look at that friend of Miss Chandler's that spoke nasty to our Susan. He's not been down since, I'll say that for him, anyway not to my knowledge. Maybe she warned him off.'

'And so I should hope! If he'd come after our Sue again I'd have bashed his face in, never mind who he is.'

'Well he didn't, so don't go on. How about those potatoes you was going to dig up for m' rabbit pie this evenin'?'

When he had left her, she tied an apron round her broad hips and sat down at the kitchen table to slice the onions and turnips he had brought in from the garden. During the whole of her married life she had worked well and methodically, with a comfortable lack of imagination. It had never seemed to her necessary to question her lot or to compare it with those who had a greater variety or more reward. Any of the larger issues which she failed to understand she abandoned with a sound philosophy: the infinite varieties of human behaviour failed to disturb her. 'There's bad *and* good,' she was wont to say, 'and I'd sooner leave it to the Lord; it's not our business. If you've done your best I reckon you can't do more.' 'Keep on the right road,' she assured Susan, 'and you won't come to no harm.'

But her young daughter was not always convinced. Returning from the local hospital, to find her mother wiping her streaming eyes over the last of the peeled onions, she sat down in the basket chair and said unsteadily: 'There was a baby died in the ward this afternoon, Mum. The doctors did all they could, and Matron was up all night ... it was ever such a dear little baby, Mum. Its mother had gone off and left it, and no one knew who its father was. It was brought in too late ... it had ever such a weak little cry.'

Mrs Bird abandoning the vegetables hastily, washed her hands at the sink and put the kettle on. 'We'll have a cup together,' she said, 'I daresay we could both do with it. And when Dad's done those spuds we'll have 'em fried for tea with a couple of sausages. Now give over crying, duck: if you're going to start training for a nurse, you'll have to get used to seeing worse things than that. I reckon the poor little baby's better off where it's gone.'

'Why did it have to happen, Mum?'

'It's not for us to question,' said Mrs Bird firmly, 'the Lord knows best—and if I could get hold of its mother, I'd call her a murderess to her face.' Having delivered herself of both satisfactory comments, she handed Susan a clean handkerchief and advised her to have a good blow.

'Miss Chandler's gone down to the sea for a week,' she said presently. 'She doesn't want any letters sent on. I reckon I'll give her place a good turn out, and Dad can clean the windows.'

'I thought he did them only last week.'

'He may have and he can do them again, once I've washed the curtains. She doesn't often go away and I reckon there's no better welcome home than nice fresh rooms.'

'You are *good*, Mum.'

'Oh I am,' returned Mrs Bird with heavy irony. 'I'm a wonder ... Come on now, lay the cloth and put out Dad's pickles.'

'Mum?'

'What is it? ... and take the piece of treacle tart out of the fridge : there's enough there for you and your father.'

'How about you then?'

'I'd sooner finish up what's left of the rice pudding we had Sunday. I might fancy a bit of strawberry jam with it. What was it you was going to say?'

'It was about Miss Chandler,' said Susan doubtfully. 'I mean, she's such a nice lady and I—I keep wondering at her being friends with—with that man.'

'You may do, and when you're a bit older you'll learn it takes all sorts to make a world. Anyway, it's not your business, nor mine, how she chooses her friends. For all we know, she may not even have seen him since that time he came down here.'

'Some of the girls at the hospital don't seem able to stop talking about men. When I was helping in the wards today they said married ones are the worst. Are they really, Mum?'

'Not the decent ones aren't. Don't you listen to what ignorant little brats go on about. I know what I'd give them if they was mine.'

'If men love their wives they wouldn't want anyone else, would they, Mum?'

Mrs Bird looked thoughtful. 'They *can* turn out funny,' she allowed, 'specially round about fifty, but it doesn't usually last. Your father had all his teeth out just about that time and I fancy it took his mind off. Anyway, I never had any trouble with him. I always say it's good for a man to have a hobby and, once he got used to his new set, he took up keeping bees.'

'Dear old Dad,' said Susan affectionately.

'You'd go a long way before you found a better,' returned her mother unexpectedly. 'And that'll do. You don't want to go worrying about Miss Chandler's friends or anyone else's. You can't live other people's lives for them, when all's said and done. You're not going to work for her so it's none of your business. And don't believe all you read in the papers neither. Decent-living people keep out of the news, and there's a lot more of them than the other sort. What I say is, it's lucky we've got a good Queen on the throne to set an example . . . Don't forget Dad's pickles.'

Susan finished laying the table, and went to stand outside in the flickering evening sunshine; the air was gentle, and the stocks edging the wet path smelled sweet. She felt soothed and comforted. Between recollections of the kitchen staff's crude chatter was her mother's solid commonsense. It took away the smear of half-comprehended dangers, it straightened the paths which lay ahead. And watching her father coming up from the little kitchen garden, with the wet rosy potatoes in a basket, she called to him softly : 'They look all right, Dad.'

'They'd better be! We've had no summer. Last year we was grousing about the heat and the drought, and this one it's bin wind and rain the whole blessèd time. Seems nothing's like it should be.'

'Were the old days better, Dad?'

'They was for some things, I reckon . . . the weather was, *and* people too . . . more what I'd call consistent . . . Oh well, I haven't got the time to go into all that now, not with your mother waiting for these spuds. Any road, setting the world to rights isn't for us to do, so we may as well leave it to them that think they can. I daresay we'll muddle through same as we've done before, right up to the end.'

'Don't you believe in progress, Dad? I do.'

'All right, duck, you go on believing in it. You've had a better education than I've had. There was a chap who joined the Navy the same time as me, what was always reading to improve himself an' quoting a bloke called Karl Marx. Didn't make much sense to me.'

'I've heard about him,' said Susan, 'he was a writer, wasn't he? I asked Mum about him and she said Miss Chandler had some of his books and seeing that he was a German, she didn't think she should.'

'And quite right too. They can keep their ideas to themselves . . . Hullo, what's that for?'

Susan gave him a second kiss. 'Because you're nice, that's why.' And when he had gone to join Mrs Bird in the kitchen, she lingered on the little porch feeling oddly happy. They were the people she knew best, who understood enough about life to make it seem orderly, to give it the cloak of kindness and the semblance of truth. It was enough for her.

'Where are you off to so bright and early?'

Alex looked with some annoyance as Elizabeth sat down

on the bench beside him at the entrance to the flats. Sunshine shone upon the round flower beds. He found their bright optimism excessive.

'I'm going down to Brighton,' he said.

'I'd heard you'd been ill.'

'People can never mind their own business,' he assured her.

'I adore Brighton. Can't I come?'

'I shouldn't think so for a moment.'

'What'll you do when you're there?'

'Sit on a balcony and do dam' all.'

'Alone and uncherished? Or mustn't I ask?'

'When do you go back to school?'

'I've left school : I was expelled.'

He looked bored. 'How very careless of you.'

'It was my last term anyhow. Do you like my new jeans?'

'I dislike the female sex of any age in trousers.'

'I could make a rather rude reply, shall I?'

'I shouldn't bother.'

'All right. How long are you going to be away?'

'I've no idea at all.'

'A boy friend of mine took me to see a blue film last night.'

'Really?' He stifled a yawn.

Elizabeth looked disappointed. 'Daddy would be furious if he knew.'

'Then you'd better not tell him.' Alex turned his head towards the gates. 'I think that's the car.'

'No, it's not, it's gone on. Do you want to get rid of me?'

'You've chosen the wrong time to pay me an unsolicited visit.'

'Why, are you tired or something? Your son's terrified of me, isn't he?'

'Sandy? You'd better take him in hand.'

'I don't like boys. I like older men.'

'You'll be getting yourself into trouble one of these days

if you don't look out.' It occurred to him that she had a very inviting smile. If everything hadn't seemed such an effort he might have suggested her coming down to lunch with him at Brighton. But he wouldn't have his own car . . . and anyhow Caroline was arriving at the week-end. He didn't feel inclined to make plans : it was easier to drift.

'When I come back,' he said, 'I'll ring you up.' After all it committed him to nothing.

'How long are you going to be away?'

'I told you before, I don't know. About two or three weeks I suppose . . . There's the car.'

The uniformed driver carried out the suitcases; he arranged the rug over his passenger's knees.

'Don't do that,' said Alex pettishly, 'and leave the window as it is.'

'Very good, sir.'

Elizabeth lingered by the open door. 'Give my love to the sea. I know a chap who's got a helicopter; if I asked him he'd bring me over.'

'Then don't ask him,' returned Alex. 'I'm going in search of a little peace and quiet.'

'How awful! I bet you'll be sick of that in five minutes.'

He was almost inclined to believe her. She looked so fresh and happy, so assured, so impudent. As the car drove away, he half wished that he had delayed it. She made him forget his fatigue, his boredom, his fear. It seemed a long time since he had had anything to which to look forward. Life had become little more than an unadventurous walk, towards no desired end. Places were repetitive, he knew them all; once he had been enthralled by a burning sun on a glittering blue sea and girls with smooth wet bodies splashing towards the hot beaches, and dance bands throbbing invitations : it was carefree, foreign, and transitory. Then there was nothing which drink could not obliterate, no memory and no dismay.

Now certainty had left him : to look back at what had been seemed pointless, he had taken what he wanted yet he felt strangely insecure, as though there was permanence nowhere. He had always prided himself on his capacity to end any episode of which he had grown tired. Luck and sophistication had been on his side. He knew what he sought and found it; to some extent, he had been assured, there was an art in that. After all, Fortune invariably smiled upon those who wooed her wisely and no sane man refused her favours.

But now, exasperated by illness, frustrated by the inability to gain strength, resigned to the knowledge that he had had his day, he sat in a corner of the hired car, angry and resentful.

'I don't know,' he told himself, 'what the devil I'm doing this for. I shall be bored stiff.'

It was Caroline's bright idea, of course, though what she got out of it he was damned if he knew. It was, in his opinion, fundamentally absurd that anyone was genuinely altruistic. There was always a catch somewhere. Presumably she simply enjoyed fostering an absurdly romantic fantasy which seemed to him quite senseless. If she had really cherished a fond feeling for him, it would have been the simplest thing in the world to have got in touch with him again. So far as he was concerned, he'd have been quite prepared to be magnanimous. He supposed she knew it, and for some masochistic reason she hadn't taken advantage of it. Some women, but she didn't appear to be one of them, adored a quarrel for the hysterical satisfaction of making it up again. But she had merely removed herself.

He had never been able to determine what she got out of her obstinacy. After all, it was only commonsense to believe that no one did anything without hope of reward. He was assured that in order to achieve a balanced view of things, a man had to make the best of every opportunity, martyrs were never an asset to any society. Only a fool would refuse to say that a man's first duty was to himself.

He pulled the discarded rug across his knees and the driver half-turning said : 'All right, sir? Would you like the window shut?'

'No,' said Alex, shortly. He closed his eyes against the formality of London's outskirts. He wanted to sleep but his mind was too restless. He wondered what the girl Elizabeth was doing. Wherever he was he wanted to be elsewhere, but the mere thought of effort was exhausting.

'I daresay I'll feel better after I've had a change of air,' he told himself. 'I'm not going to pack up yet.'

Chapter Twelve

'GOT YOURSELF a job, have you?' enquired the flats' porter with easy familiarity.

'You could say that,' returned Elizabeth, leaning against the door to watch him polish the windows. 'You don't suppose I left school for the pleasure of living at home and watching my venerable mother play bridge all the afternoon and half the night, do you?'

'What's your father got to say to that?'

'Daddy? He couldn't care less. He calls himself a member of the Bar but most of the time the only bar he props up is at his Club, drowning his sorrows over his racing debts.'

'He gave me a tip for the St Leger once.'

'Did you take it?'

'Not me, I'd sooner risk anything I've got on the dogs. You're back early, aren't you? You work at that posh florist place round the corner, don't you?'

'Put it in the past tense.'

'Come again. Would you mean you've got the sack?'

'Well to be exact, I walked out.'

'Didn't you like it then? You haven't been there more than the fortnight, have you?'

'Ten days. The manageress was a bitch. She kept all the male customers to herself, and told me to scram at first sight of a bowler hat.'

'I guess they'd have been too old for you. They was

probably buying flowers for their wives.'

'Be your age! Chaps don't send orchids to their wives.'

'You know the lot, don't you!' He flapped his leathers and grinned. 'When my young sister started talking like that my father soon put a stop to it. "One more word," he said "and I'll give you a hiding you won't forget in a hurry." '

'Why? It wasn't his business.'

'He thought it was, anyway. He's an ex-policeman, brought us all up very strict. Not that I blame him.'

'Are you married?'

'Going to be at Christmas. Well, I must get on else I'll never get this lot finished.'

She was surprised to be dismissed so casually. Always she wanted to test her powers of enticement, it did not matter with whom. She was excitable and impatient, and unselective. It amused her to lead a man on for the fun of the thing; she had no desire to be kind; nor was it in her nature to be generous. She watched plays on the screen and came to regard violence, sensationalism, and greed as a true reflection of the common trend. She laughed at little cruelties, at the debasing of pride, at the larger issues of brutality. There was no necessity to pause, no time to think, all that mattered was a swift passage from one excitement to another.

When the hall porter had gone away with his buckets and his leathers she strolled slowly out of the quadrangle and into the street. In the exhilaration of quitting her job she had forgotten to ring anyone up to tell them the glad news. They might not be particularly interested, but no one objected to a little celebration.

At the moment she could not think of any friends whom she would be glad to see, but that didn't matter; after a few drinks most people were happy to celebrate anything. And anyway, she was not inviting them as a matter of altruism :

133

they were stop-gaps to boredom, and tomorrow was another day.

A long grey car had slowed down by the curb at her side; the head thrust out of the window was dark and sleek. 'Can you tell me the way to Marylebone Station, please?'

'Give me time and I expect I can,' said Elizabeth.

The car door opened. 'Why not get in if it's going to take so long?'

For a moment she hesitated. The voice, silky, too careful for an Englishman, seemed somehow at variance with something at once shifty and watchful in the sallow face. He might, she told herself, be a waiter—or a foreign diplomat. His long fingers resting on the handle of the car, were smooth and flexible.

Well, after all, there was no reason why she shouldn't get in and study a map with him. He might even change his mind about going to Marylebone Station, and drive her somewhere for a drink.

I can take care of myself, Elizabeth told herself.

Caroline wrapped a warm bath towel round the small protesting Rosie and lifted her on to her lap.

'I don't want to get out yet.'

'It's getting late, Rosie, and you'll be too sleepy to eat your banana and cream unless we hurry.'

'Why will I?'

'Because it's almost seven o'clock and all the birds have gone to bed.'

'Why have they?'

'Because they've got to wake up early tomorrow morning and sing.'

'I can sing : at school I sing louder than anyone.'

'Do you like Nursery School, Rosie?'

'No. It's silly ... When's Mummy coming back?'

'When Daddy brings her home from the party.'

'I want her *now*.'

'I've got something in the next room for you.'

'What is it?'

'Wait until you've got your nighty on.'

'Why must I?'

The ceaseless questions, the frank self-absorption, the casual innocence seemed exhausting, but the little face with its enquiring smile, the soft hair gathered into an absurd knot, the round arms circling Caroline's neck gave her an amused pleasure, with all its limitations perhaps the only untainted delight remaining.

'Where's my present?'

'It's only a very little one, Rosie.'

'I don't mind.'

Gratitude, the inadequate response for the gifts of life, it seemed to her could never be truly taught until sorrow had dug its pit. To teach a child to be grateful for what it had received, was a simplification; to expect from maturity a gracious reception of the harsher truths of experience seemed optimistic. Caroline certainly didn't expect it. But at least she had knowledge of the remedial effect of pain, and she could lower her pride to accept it, without in any way diminishing the integrity of her nature.

'Where is it?' asked Rosie, skipping into the nursery.

'Where is what?' asked Caroline, hanging the pink bath towels over the radiator to dry.

'What you said you was going to give me.'

'It's a very little present, Rosie. It's not your birthday or Christmas, is it?'

'You did *promise*.' The small chin quivered dangerously.

'Of course I did. Hop into bed.' Caroline took a little paper bag from her satchel and drew out a blue sugar mouse.

Rosie beamed. 'Fank you,' she said, 'I like him, he's nice.

I'll show him to our pussy but I won't let her eat him because he's mine.'

'Shall we put him on the little table beside you before you go to sleep?'

'No, he wants to be with me.' She snuggled down and murmured : 'Are you going home now?'

'No, I'm staying here with you until your Mummy comes back.'

'Yes.'

There, Caroline recognized, was a satisfied confidence and it seemed to her enough. She had a respect for the good sense of children which was quite unsentimental. She knew that Rosie's parents were practical, affectionate, and self-absorbed. They were, in her opinion, among the better products of a type not afflicted by any exaggerated ideas of service. They made light-hearted use of their acquaintances, they were casually hospitable, and not conspicuously loyal. To them friendship was fun demanding no strictures.

Caroline was interested in a point of view she saw no possibility of sharing. The young in an age in which she had grown old admitted nothing from choice that might prove hampering to prized individuality. They were people in their own right. The insecurity of the future cast no shadow upon their paths.

Caroline looking back at her own lost years, wondered again if she had abandoned recklessly all risk of happiness, all danger of delight for the selfishness of principle. Other people managed these things so much better than she did, or took them more lightly.

The child stirred and stood up, her eyes closed, clutching the sugar mouse.

'Do you want to get out, Rosie?'

Enthroned on a plastic chamber-pot, she murmured sleepily : 'Come another day.'

136

'I will. Not tomorrow because I'm going to the sea.'

'Why?' But reposing again on her pillow, she was asleep before there was time for an answer.

The elderly night porter looked at the thick watch on his wrist: ten minutes to go, and then he could lock up and shuffle down to the basement flat where his wife was already preparing his cup of cocoa. There were not many tenants who kept late hours in this block and he was glad of it. There was the lady who played bridge night after night but she always got rid of her visitors before her husband came back from the Club, and he didn't blame her, seeing that the chap, for all he was one of the high-ups at the Bar, couldn't walk straight nor think straight by the time he got in. *She* was all right, though the day porter said she neglected her young daughter shameful, with her bridge and that.

'About time that girl was back,' muttered the night porter, 'else she'll find herself locked out. I'll have something to say to her if she gets me out of my bed after me and the wife have got cosy. It's not part of my job to let 'em in, not in the small hours of the morning.'

He opened a tin of bull's-eyes and sucked one slowly. The evening paper was neatly folded ready for the wife to lay the fire in their room in the morning. There was nothing in his view to beat coal for comfort . . . Outside everything was quiet, a distant clock chimed midnight.

'All right my girl, you've had it,' muttered the porter, and took up his keys.

'Can't you lay still for goodness sake,' complained Mr Bird. 'You've tossed and turned enough times. Is your stomach upsettin' you or something? Why didn't you tell me an' I'd have got you your salts. They'd soon settle it.'

'You go to sleep,' returned his wife, 'I'm all right, I don't need anything.'

137

E*

'Well, if you've flung yourself about over nothing, stop it and give us both a bit of rest.'

'It was just a bit I was reading about in the paper, how there's a crime committed every hour or something. I can't help thinking of their mothers.'

'Whose mothers, for goodness sake? What's come over you? Suppose there *is* crime an' all that, in the world, it doesn't help to keep on about it. It's not our trouble.'

'I only hope our Susan finds a good man to look after her when the time comes.'

'There you go again! Anyone would think you was half way to forbidding the banns before the girl's s'much as met the one she likes. What are you fussing about? You stop reading the stuff they put in the papers. I reckon half of it's lies. Come on, give us a smacker, and shut up.'

'I don't know what kind of set me off,' said Mrs Bird apologetically, and dabbed a repentant kiss on his cheek, 'but it makes you wonder sometimes, even if you'd sooner not.'

'Yes, well move over a bit, you're laying on me bunion and you're not as light as you once was, m'old dear! I daresay there's reasons for most things if we was to know. Maybe it's as well we don't. And I don't suppose we'd understand any better if we did.'

Chapter Thirteen

SHE HAD grown so used to the sensation of belonging to no one that she had had little, if any, awareness of self-importance. The small events and distractions of her daily life had caused time to slide away from her almost imperceptibly. The liberty which came from a lack of attachment to people lent her a wry dignity, and she had no desire to enlist sympathy for her solitary state.

Looking back, it seemed to Caroline that her life had been sufficiently orderly until Alex had come to disrupt it. Her short-lived affair with the young airman, in her extreme youth, had made her feel a little sorry that he should have mistaken her gentle acquiescence for a warmth to match his own. In seducing her he had supposed that they had come to the beginning of the affair and not the end. She had not intended to bewilder him but her inexperience had taught her little tact. She always hoped that his hurt pride did not endure.

For her part she considered it unnecessary to attach any importance to the episode. But when she had grown up to a better regard for herself, she became too confident of her immunity. Caught in the meshes of a love beyond reason and commonsense, she had learnt her bitter lesson. Even now, all these years after, she felt again the clutch of sorrow which had given her so much pain. And yet, with deliberation, she was walking towards the source of all her distress, conscious that he needed her and that in his need, she might be of use.

As she sat at the window of the hotel bedroom, overlooking a sullen sea, her spirits drooped. He had asked her to meet him in the lounge downstairs at half-past four. He had sounded unamiable and abrupt on the telephone, complaining that she had not arrived in time to lunch with him, that his room was overheated and the corridors worse. He added that he had forgotten to order a morning paper. When he rang off, it seemed to Caroline that she would have her work cut out attempting to cheer him. Presently she went down the thickly carpeted stairs and walked into a lounge whose heavy crimson curtains were already drawn : large upholstered armchairs were occupied by large elderly women seated opposite round tables containing little china teapots, covered dishes of muffins, and slices of chocolate cake. Caroline felt more depressed than ever.

'I couldn't agree with you more,' said Alex.

She turned to greet him. 'How awful of me! Does it really show?'

'Horribly,' he assured her, and led the way to a small table in an alcove. 'Why didn't you come this morning?'

'I couldn't, I was having my hair done.'

'So I gathered. It looks rather nice . . . By way of terrific dissipation they turn on a coloured television after dinner. Does the idea attract you?'

'Not very much. Can't one read in here?'

'What an unsociable woman you are . . . What'll you have, crumpets or buttered toast?'

He looked, she thought, better than she had expected. His ill-humour appeared to have vanished.

'You'll probably be asked to play bridge,' he told her presently. 'They tried it on with me, but I refused so emphatically that I think—and hope—I've made enemies for life.'

'I can't play, so there's a pair of us.'

'How very satisfactory of you, Caroline. We can sit and talk together in my room till the small hours. We shall possibly get turned out in the morning but you must take the risk.'

'Would they really, at my age?'

'Don't be absurd, of course they would. Let's try it and see.'

'I'd rather not, I've booked for the week-end.'

'What a mercenary woman you are! That's not your real reason though, is it?'

'Yes.'

'I don't believe you. Well, you've only just arrived so we won't quarrel. Tomorrow we'll walk together up the promenade and take enormous gulps of sea air. After which we'll hire a car and lunch elsewhere. We might even go to a cinema afterwards.'

'Don't you rest in the afternoon?'

'No, I refuse to be treated like an invalid.'

'Perfectly healthy people rest after lunch. I always do.'

'You go to bed?'

'No, I lie in a chair and pretend to read.'

'Do you have someone to do your housework for you? Oh yes, I remember, you do. She had a pretty little blue-eyed daughter who ran away from me in terror. I thought they were more sophisticated than that nowadays.'

'Not all of them. Her parents take great care of Susan.'

'That sort usually break out all the more. I must confess I am distinctly bored by the present-day young, aren't you?'

'I see so little of them. I like what I hear of their independence and determination not to be a drag on their parents.'

'What about their morals?'

'Again I don't know enough about them to express an opinion. I suppose most of them take life lightly. I'm not at all sure that isn't quite a good thing.'

'That wasn't your experience, was it?'

'Perhaps not.'

The large women in the cushioned chairs were watching Caroline with the curiosity of the idle. Living in sea coast hotels, undistracted by household cares, they passed the winter of their years in affluence and boredom. It was difficult to imagine that they had ever suffered traumatic injury or endured the wreckage of unwisdom.

'I know exactly what you're thinking about,' Alex told her.

'I hope not : it was rather uncharitable.'

'Incidentally, Caroline, why aren't you eating?'

'I'm not hungry.'

'Would that be necessary? How little you've changed! When did you give up your job with the eminent solicitors?'

'About ten years ago. The partner I knew best died, he was a nice old thing, and I felt it was time I stopped being one of the world's workers.'

'Did you loathe it?'

'My work? No. It was a harmless occupation and enabled me to save a little money.'

'You're possessed of a contented nature.'

'No, a philosophic one.'

'Am I expected to believe that?'

'I don't see why not.'

He pushed aside his tea-cup. 'Do you mind if I smoke one of my rationed cigars? By the way, I looked up my heart specialist before coming down here, not for any better reason than sheer curiosity. He's a nice fellow and told me a couple of extremely amusing stories which are not for your delicate ears. When I saw him in the nursing home he was much less *bon garçon* than he was in his own consulting room.'

'Did he find you better, Alex?'

'As a matter of fact, he did. He said I looked as if I'd taken on a new lease of life and, of course, took all credit to himself. So in order to take him down a peg or two, I told him my improvement was largely due to you.'

'I'm not expected to believe that one, am I?'

'Please yourself. He's by way of being a bit of a psychologist and agreed entirely with me that I needed someone to take an interest in me. And what better than the emergence of a lost love?'

'Didn't you tell him you've never at any time lacked anyone to take interest in you?'

'I did not. I should take umbrage, Caroline, at that most uncalled-for remark were it not that you're on the brink of tears. It's no use trying to disguise the fact. And I'll give you the reason if you like. You're uncommonly glad that I'm not in danger of immediate extinction. Aren't you now?'

'Of course I am, Alex, bless you. Very, very glad.'

'There's a frightful risk attached to all this you know,' he told her. 'We might fall in love all over again.'

'Nonsense.' And she hoped very much that she sounded convincing.

'I dunno what they'll expect next, sitting up the whole blasted night, waiting till breakfast time and then the little devil never turned up. Kept my missus awake too. They won't catch me doing it again, I can tell you,' complained the night porter.

'Well you got a fiver out of it anyway,' said the day porter soothingly.

'I may have, that's not the point. I'm not here to be made use of. I've got m' duty to do, and I do it, but I'm not a blasted nursemaid, an' if youngsters like to spend the night out, it's not part of my job to sit up for 'em. Her mother wasn't half in a state neither : come out in her dressing gown two or three times, creating. I wonder the other tenants didn't hear her. I thought she'd call the police the way she went on. Her husband had a job to quiet her. Not that he was all that sober himself.

'Wouldn't have been him if he had been, I reckon. Mind you, I like the chap when he's not too blind to speak sensible. If you ask me, that girl's never had much of a chance, not the way she's been left to bring herself up. I hope nothing's happened to her. It wouldn't surprise me. Been to posh schools and all. It just shows money's not everything. Her mother was telephoning around to all their friends to find out if she's stopped the night with any of them, so she told me this morning when I took her papers in. She looked a sight, I can tell you, without all that stuff on her face. Well, I'm going to have m' breakfast an' get off to my bed. I reckon I've earned it . . . you should have seen the way his hand was shaking when he passed me the fiver.'

'That's nothing new. Still, I daresay he's worried. In his own way, I fancy he's fond of the girl. I hope she turns up all right. She's only a kid when all's said and done.'

Left to himself, the younger man collected the rest of the morning papers and thrust them through the appropriate letter boxes. He greeted the postman with rather less than his accustomed jollity but something restrained him from mentioning Elizabeth. 'Seems funny to me,' he told himself, 'very funny.'

Presently the male tenants in bowler hats and neat suits shouldered their umbrellas and marched away to their cars or to the underground. Two or three young women, with superior faces and admirable clothes, hurried through the hall. The day had begun.

At half-past nine a square-shouldered, florid man, his thin plastered hair combed off a hot forehead, crossed the hall and said abruptly : 'Tell our daily when she comes in not to disturb my wife; she's just taken a sleeping pill.'

'Very good, sir.'

'The fact is my young daughter forgot to tell us she was spending the night away ... the snag is we don't know where ... Did you take a suitcase down for her yesterday by any chance?'

'No, sir.'

'You don't happen to remember what time she left, or didn't you see her?'

'I reckon it might have been round about two or half-past. I saw the Major being fetched soon after his lunch. But I saw her a bit later on because I call to mind I was finishing the windows I'd had to leave on account of the rain in the morning.'

'Was she going out, did you happen to notice?'

'I wouldn't have said so, sir, she hadn't a coat on when I saw her. Kind of standing by the doors, to see if the rain had stopped.'

'Of course one of her friends may have called for her, and she forgot to let us know where she'd gone.'

'Yes, sir. I was doing the windows at the back so I wouldn't have seen her go.'

'Quite ... So she didn't tell you she was likely to be late?'

'No, sir.'

'If she'd met with an accident, the police would have let us know.'

'That's right, sir.'

'Yes ... I'm not going up to Chambers this morning. I'd better not leave my wife ... she's had to put off her bridge ... she's not well, you know. It's her nerves.'

'I'm sorry, sir. Will you be sending for the doctor?'

'That's an idea ... I don't quite know what excuse I could give ... the fact is I'm not feeling too brilliant myself. I think I'll leave it for a bit ... I might ring at lunch time ... I suppose Miss Elizabeth didn't give you any idea where she was going? No, of course, I asked you that before ... I'm not at my best as early as this ... I don't know why my daughter didn't take some things for the night, but I believe they think nothing of borrowing from friends if they stay on the spur of the moment, extraordinary way to live, but they will do it.'

'Suits them, I reckon.'

'It doesn't do to interfere, you know.' He paused, as if questioning his own garrulity, and went on : 'They know their way about in these days. You can't live their lives for them. You married?'

'Going to be at Christmas.'

'My advice to you is don't. If I had my time over again, I wouldn't. If you ask me, there's nothing to be gained from it.'

'I wouldn't say that, sir.'

'There speaks the voice of ignorance : you wait ... some people of course *do* have luck ... but for most of us it's a mug's game.'

The young porter watched him as he wandered away. 'I know if I had a daughter that had gone missing, I wouldn't sit at home drowning m' troubles,' he muttered, 'I'd go after her and raise merry hell till I got her back.' In the simplicity of his heart, he believed in the straight lines he had been brought up to follow. His theories were primitive, his desire for direct action seemed right. Those who claimed to be his elders and betters only won his respect if he found them in his own class. The tenants who occupied the expensive flats, whose windows he washed and whose door-knobs he polished, aroused his amiable contempt. He wore the uniform of the place, he opened and closed car doors, and, on the whole, he kept his opinions to himself. But he was not hoodwinked by affluence or the assertive rights of the well-to-do. He understood what seemed to him to be obvious and dismissed the rest. He would do what he had to do, hang on to the job and marry his girl. Presently he would try for more remunerative work, and move into a council flat, and have a couple of kids. And his wife, being in his view the right sort, would stay at home and look after the three of them.

'I reckon that's what a home's for,' he decided. 'I dunno but I don't seem able to get that young Elizabeth out of my head. I know I'd go bonkers if I'd a daughter what stopped out all night ... I wonder where the hell she's got to ... regular little madam she is, but I must say I'd be glad to see her back, churns you up thinking of what might have happened.'

Chapter Fourteen

MR BIRD tethered by a short length of cotton while his wife secured a button on his shirt cuff, breathed heavily through his nose. 'That'll do. I shan't pull that off easy,' he said impatiently.

'Don't fidget else you'll get pricked and whose fault will that be?' retorted Mrs Bird. 'I'd sooner leave a job than not do it properly. I dunno how you'd ever get on if I wasn't here to see to you.'

'Now don't you start off on that! If I've told you once I've told you a dozen times, I don't like it. You've no call to talk about pushing up the daisies at your age.'

Snapping the cotton between her teeth, she buttoned his cuff and put her needle back in its case. 'There you are,' she said, 'and don't keep on pulling your shirt over your head without you undo it properly; there's no need to hurry at bedtime.'

'That's what *you* say, my duck,' retorted Mr Bird, at which she shook her head with a reluctant smile and looked flattered.

'Funny thing,' said his wife, when they were sitting beside the wood fire in the parlour, 'Miss Chandler's telephone went when I was ironing her curtains this morning, 'course she told me to answer if anyone rung up an' put it on the pad. I'd a job to hear because it was from London . . .'

'That shouldn't make no difference, not if it was from

Warsaw if the line was clear,' he interrupted. 'We'll have to get your mum a hearing-aid, shan't we, Sue?'

His daughter smiled at the pair of them a little absently; she sat in a corner of the old leather sofa with a small manual on Home Nursing in her hand and a pucker on her smooth forehead.

'Stop chattering when someone else is speaking,' reproved Mrs Bird. 'I can hear as well as the next person when they speak up. Anyway, they asked for Miss Chandler, an' wouldn't leave no message bar to ask when she'd be back. Didn't leave no name neither; it was a gentleman speaking and he said he'd ring again tomorrow.'

'It wouldn't have been that prize specimen that was visiting down here and run after our Sue? ... It's all right, girl, you needn't colour up. I'd soon settle *him* ...'

'No, it wasn't him,' replied Mrs Bird. 'The gentleman said something about his wife wanting to have a word, but seeing Miss Chandler was away, it 'ud have to wait. Struck me he sounded kind of upset, it might have been the line, of course ... I reckon Miss Chandler will be pleased with her curtains, they've come up lovely.'

'Dad,' said Susan, 'what's resuscitate mean?'

'Well,' said Mr Bird, sucking his teeth thoughtfully, 'I fancy it means throw-up, but I wouldn't take a bet on it. Ask your mother.'

'What are you reading then?' demanded Mrs Bird. 'I don't see what they want to use words like that for in First Aid, or whatever it is you're after. I'd sooner they was practical and got on with it.'

'I *think*,' said Susan tentatively, 'it means reviving somebody.'

'Well, why couldn't they have said so in the first place?' demanded her father. 'They *would* have to try and make it complicated. I reckon your mother's as good a nurse as any, and we never had none of this palaver when you was little.'

'I remember Mum nursing us that time we all had the mumps,' said Susan, smiling at Mrs Bird. 'I only hope I'm as good when I start work in the Children's Ward.'

'You'll do all right,' returned Mrs Bird, 'don't you worry.'

'How about a spot of praise for *me*?' enquired her husband. 'I mind when one of our boys bashed his nose playing football on the Green, and no one couldn't stop it bleeding till I come along and dropped the back door key down his back and done the trick in a jiffy.'

'Yes, well, you let Sue get on with her reading, and we'll hear the story of how you saved your son's life in the nick of time, another evening. I reckon it'll keep, seeing we've heard it half a dozen times already.'

'Hark at her!' said Mr Bird. 'I wonder I stand for it.'

Susan looked from one to the other with love, pride, and understanding.

'I wonder what they wanted Miss Chandler on the telephone for,' said her mother, 'it's been on my mind all day.'

'I wish I knew what we'll be doing this time next year,' said Sandy.

'Joining the ranks of the unemployed,' said the younger of his two study companions cheerfully. 'You'll be at Cambridge of course, well on the road to ruin, scoffing drugs and all the rest of it. Or taking Holy Orders and joining the fairies.'

'Oh, *shut* up,' complained Sandy. 'Anyhow, they're not all like that.' He looked at the grinning pair with exasperation. They were always ragging him and making him feel a fool.

'There *are* alternatives,' said the younger boy. 'My brother told me about a chap on his staircase who smuggled a girl into his room and let her out in the morning by the simple expedient of a little roof climbing and what-have-you. No one was any the wiser. Great show.'

Sandy never knew whether to believe them or not. He was going through a romantic phase of which he was half ashamed and which he had no desire to reveal to anyone. Occasionally he wrote verses and speedily destroyed them. He had an idea that they were no worse and no better than any other boy's efforts. But they gave him a slightly confused pleasure which he would have found it difficult to define.

He was no longer upset by the cheerfully lewd conversation around him, it was merely familiar and boring. He did not want to giggle about sex—he preferred to be grave, even tearful, about love which seemed to him suitable if it ended in tragedy.

'I do hope, darling,' his mother said during the holidays, 'you won't let yourself become at all *morbid*. Some of the great poets are so sad. Of course, I've always found the Lake District very debilitating myself.'

'Aren't they trying to cook up something about Wordsworth and his sister, or have I got it wrong?' asked Tom cheerfully. 'Seems to me they can't leave anyone snug in their graves. I must say I think it's rather bad form when the fellow's not here to defend himself. Of course, precious few people give a damn for reticence nowadays but I'm bound to admit I think it's a mistake. I can't say I see the point of dragging everything into the limelight. Let sleeping dogs lie.'

'I do so agree with you, Tom dear,' said Milly. 'Wordsworth wrote such nice poems. I remember one I learnt when I was a little girl at school called "To A Butterfly". It was so sweet.'

Sandy recalled that he had walked out of the room : his mother's gentle inanities made him feel as impatient as the incessant libidinous talk at school irritated him. He was not sure which side he was on, he only knew that neither satisfied the urge to get away from it all. Verses formed in his mind, secretly cherished, which seemed to express something elusive and tantalizing. There they hung, with no foundation on which to build, no coherence to soothe his excited imagination. The search for ease eluded all his groping. Everything seemed to slip away from him directly he drew near : he despised the distractions he might have obtained, his mother's loving foolishness, his step-father's jolly incomprehension, the jocose comments of his friends. Somewhere, in some hidden place, were the faint sounds which one day might be his to bring to birth, and he could find that undiscovered beauty and learn to be a poet.

'There's no necessity to follow me about the whole dam' time,' Alex told her. 'I'm perfectly capable of strolling into the town by myself. D'you think I'm going to make a round of the pubs or something?'

'No,' said Caroline, 'but it *is* a quarter of a mile's stroll to the tobacconist's shop and—oddly enough—a quarter of a mile back . . .'

'Don't be indulgent with me : I hate it.'

They sat in the doubtful warmth of the hotel's sun room, while the teasing wind shook the windows and a grey sea splashed little angry waves against the foam-flecked shingle.

'What possible good this place is supposed to do me, I can't imagine,' he continued.

'It's a change of scene and the food's rather good. You said yourself you were sleeping much better.'

'I feel violently irritable.'

'That, of course, is a pity.'

'Don't laugh, Caroline.'

'Why not? I enjoy the opportunity.'

His face changed and grew kinder. 'Don't you often laugh?'

'When I can.'

'That's no answer.' He pulled himself up and took her hand. 'Come along, put your coat on, since you obviously think I'm not to be trusted in the town alone. You imagine I'll spoil the good work by having a booze-up, don't you?'

'Not really,' she said, 'you're too sensible.'

He checked her as they were leaving the draughty room. 'Whichever way one looks at it,' he said, 'I haven't brought you much happiness, have I? I can't see what you get out of it all.'

'Come along, otherwise that shop will be closed for their lunch hour.'

'Why do you do it, Caroline?'

'I don't think I know the answer to that one.'

'Do you want me to attribute that to cowardice?'

'I expect so.'

'In other words because you're still fond of me?'

'Your powers of deduction do you infinite credit,' she retorted.

'Actually,' he said, as they walked into the hotel's front garden, 'it's more than that, isn't it? For some unknown reason it always has been, I suppose. The thing that's so infuriating is that you don't give me credit for anything on my part. Don't you want that?'

'Alex, I can't battle with this wind and talk sense at the same time.'

'That's an excuse. It's not a land wind, it's a sea wind. All we're getting is a relatively gentle breeze.'

Crossing the pebble-strewn path, he took her arm and steered her towards the little asphalt promenade and the iron bars which separated them from the strewn beach and the sucking sea.

'It seems to me quite senseless to waste any more time,' he said; 'at our age we can't afford to squander it. We might as well make the most of what's left. I feel better directly I see you, and I've come to the rather obvious conclusion that I want you with me all the time. There may not be much more of it.'

'And if there was?'

'All the better.'

She gazed at the encroaching waves carrying their little burdens of flotsam towards the shore. I'm not sure,' she said slowly, 'that I could take a—a renewal of unhappiness. I'm too old.'

'Why the hell *should* you be unhappy? What are you talking about, Caroline? We're not a pair of young, passionate lovers, we're on the last lap, both of us. What in Heaven's name is to prevent us enjoying it as best we can? Are you afraid that there'll be too much for you to do? I'm perfectly prepared to exchange my flat for one capable of housing the pair of us.'

'I'm very fond of my home, and I love the country. I don't want to leave it.'

'You're creating difficulties on purpose ... Why did you shiver, are you cold?'

'A little.'

'All right, let's go on walking. We'll stroll to the top and then back. Look here, Caroline, if we got quietly married in London and settled down together, everything would be perfectly easy. You know, it's an extraordinary thing but you seem to bring me an odd sense of security. I've hated feeling ill when I've been on my own. All the nursing homes gave me was their damned impersonal efficiency.'

'Which was what you needed, more than anything.'

'Rot. You don't understand—or you're being wilfully blind. What other woman would have been—what's the word—*constant* all these years?'

'But it wasn't a particularly welcome gift, was it? Be honest, Alex, you forgot me quite easily.'

'No, I didn't. You made me incredibly angry; in my mind I trumped up every possible argument against you. I got an absurd satisfaction in being unfaithful to you . . .'

'You could hardly call it that, I wasn't your wife.'

'But you loved me. I knew that and I had an entirely irrational desire to make you pay for having humiliated me. Obviously you'd never know about the various women I had, but I hoped my marriage with Milly would hurt you. And when that collapsed, I told myself that if you got to hear about it, you'd say it was no more than I deserved.'

'No. I didn't think that. I was sorry for both of you.'

'To hell with that, and anyhow your pity was wasted on Milly. She's got all she wanted. The woman's a fool anyway.'

'Doesn't Sandy mean anything to you, Alex?'

'No, why should he? Don't be sentimental about him, Caroline. I've got no sort of feeling for him at all, it would be sheer hypocrisy to pretend that I have. It's quite obvious that he doesn't like me, which no doubt is Milly's doing and, from the very little that I heard of that fool Garland, I'm sure he fulfils the parental rôle quite satisfactorily.'

They walked on in silence while the shrill wind whistled about their ears, and the petulant sea splashed against the breakwaters.

'Why drag in Sandy?' he asked presently.

'I suppose it was rather silly.'

'You know, Caroline, your capacity for seeing the other person's point of view is ridiculous,' he complained, 'and rather sweet, though, as a matter of fact, I'm not sure that it's quite genuine. You do it for the sake of avoiding an argument, don't you?'

'Not entirely.'

'Tell me, quite honestly, don't you really think it would be a good idea if we got married?'

'Not very; and when you're reasonably well again, I don't think you'd like it much either.'

'There you're wrong. In the first place I doubt my ever being really fit again, better perhaps, but more or less of a semi-invalid. I'm not offering you much, am I?'

'That's a matter of opinion.'

'Be that as it may, will you take the risk?'

'Alex, I must think it over. We both must. I'm not at all sure, as I told you before, that I could take a renewal of strain and I think that would be almost bound to happen. Listen, it's quite true that I do love you, very much . . .'

'Bless you, of course you do. You sound like yourself now. And whether you believe me or not, I'm fonder of you than I've ever been of any woman. I really mean that. I know you tried to root me out of your life, but you couldn't manage it, could you?'

'I think I'd rather we didn't talk about it any more at present. Let's just go into the town and get your cigarettes, and then go back to the hotel.'

'Why, are you tired?'

'Yes, and so are you.'

'When we're married you'll spoil me outrageously.'

'I don't think you'd enjoy that very much, Alex. You don't know yourself awfully well, do you?'

'I don't suppose you'd overdo it.'

A reluctant sun came out to gild the neat row of little shops on the edge of the town. A few elderly men, muffled against the wind, walked with uncertain haste across the red-tiled pavements; a few elderly women, morose in expensive tweed coats and carrying pet dogs, hurried with small quick steps towards a café and the scent of hot chocolate.

'Caroline,' said Alex, watching them, 'be warned.'

She laughed. 'It's all right. I'm too poor, and I'm much fonder of small children than toy poodles.'

'Children, are you? I never knew that. Somehow it doesn't seem to fit into the picture.'

'I don't follow you.'

'You're a sentimentalist by nature I suppose. One could, of course, suggest that you've got a tender heart.'

'Thank you.'

'I should prefer to have an exclusive right to it.'

She said nothing : she wanted to go indoors, to the un-familiar hotel bedroom, to be by herself, to turn on the elec-tric fire, take off her shoes and rest.

'If I were on my own,' he said, when he had pocketed his cigarettes, 'I should now find a likely pub. As it is, I shall obey my new doctor's instructions and restrict myself to the permitted brandy and soda at lunch. I wonder how long I shall keep up the good work. It largely depends on you, of course.'

'I don't think I like blackmail, Alex.'

'That's not a very nice way of putting it, you rude woman ... Caroline, don't go back to your damned cottage tomor-row.'

'I must, really. Apart from anything else, I want to think things over.'

'No you don't. I shall go back myself in a day or two and start arrangements.'

'You mustn't rush me, Alex.'

'I intend to. It's the only way of dealing with you. You know you love it really.'

'Not at my age.'

'Blast your age, Caroline : anyhow I'm older than you are and think it's very tactless of you to harp on the subject ...

Good! You're laughing. You know, we're going to have great fun together ... Hold on a moment, d'you still like roses?'

They stood outside the narrow window of the little florist against whose misty panes was the blur of expensive flowers standing in tall vases.

'Alex, they'll be ruinous.'

'All the better.' He pushed open the door and led her in. The little place smelled of damp mould and sweet scent.

'Can I help you, sir?'

'Give me a dozen of those,' he said, and stared at the slender girl as she took the long-stemmed roses from the window. She was very cool and very pretty, including Caroline in her attractive professional smile. She saw him glance at the name of the place, painted in black lettering upon the little signboard.

'Here you are,' he said, when they were outside, and put the flowers into Caroline's hand.

'Thank you, dear Alex, they're perfectly lovely.'

'They'll cheer your place up tomorrow.'

She did not know whether he was deliberately ceasing to deplore talk of her departure, or if he had merely forgotten about it. After all, what did it matter, the result was the same.

When she reached her room, she turned on the fire, shivering a little in her greatcoat, and put the flowers in water. She wished that he had not given them to her.

Chapter Fifteen

'WELL THERE'S one thing for sure,' declared Mrs Bird, 'we was put into this world to help others, and it's a pity more doesn't remember it. I wouldn't say I'm exactly what you'd call *religious* but I hope I know my duty, and seeing that I told Miss Chandler I was always ready to help out in an emergency, so long as it's only kind of temporary . . .'

'Yes, well, you be careful,' advised Mr Bird, 'I've known temporary turn out permanent, behind your back, and then act real nasty if you was to say that wasn't the arrangement.'

'Mebbe some do and some don't. I reckon friends of Miss Chandler's wouldn't act so deceitful. The few times I been over to their flat when she's asked me after they've given a little party, and I've helped with the washing up, they've always behaved very fair over the money, and he's never made any trouble driving me back in his car even if he's had to go a bit careful on account of not feeling all that steady.'

'I wonder Miss Chandler troubles with them,' grumbled Mr Bird, 'seeing they're not really her sort. I reckon she acts a bit too charitable sometimes to my way of thinking.'

'It's no business of yours or mine if she does,' declared his wife briskly. 'Live and let live, that's what I say. To tell the honest truth I don't think much of either of them meself, but I'm sorry for the boy and if I can do something for him, now and then, in a little way, I'm pleased to do it.'

'You're too soft-hearted, that's what you are,' said Mr Bird, 'anyone can get round you, go the proper way about it . . .'

'There's no call for you both to stop at home,' Mrs Bird had assured Milly. 'You don't want to put off going up to London, seeing it's your birthday and he's took the theatre tickets and all. Mr Sandy won't mind coming over to us for his dinner, I don't suppose. We've a rabbit pie, and I reckon he'd not say no to a treacle pudding. My Susan's at home and she can cut up his dinner for him. And if you was to drop him at our place round about twelve on your way out, and fetch him in the evening when you get back, you won't have nothing to worry about.'

'It's so *very* kind of you,' began Milly, with deplorable hesitancy, 'if it wasn't for the fact that my husband would be so disappointed if we didn't go . . .'

'And rightly, to my way of thinking. You don't have to trouble about it at all, you go and enjoy yourselves for once. I don't fancy Mr Sandy minds missing going up to the theatre, not with his wrist broke and all. He'd sooner stay quiet at home. He's not one to complain of missing school neither !'

Milly looked slightly offended. 'He's got three "A" levels, you know.'

'That's right, he told me he had. Of course sometimes the other boys take it out of the clever ones, ragging as they call it and that.'

'He's at a very civilized school,' said Milly, with the certainty of complete ignorance, 'and it was nobody's fault that he fell in the gymnasium.'

'Well, he don't weigh all that much, not to fall heavy. Perhaps he was tripped up. I know boys.'

Milly sighed. She was inclined to doubt Mrs Bird's knowledge of public school 'men' who, according to Sandy, were very much less barbarous than they used to be. Devoted though she was to her son, she could not help wishing that he would remain at school during his last term without either falling sick or injuring himself. Tom, of course, was perfectly good-natured about it, and merely made cheerful jokes about Sandy's minor misfortunes which were something of a relief to Milly, since she could not resist the impression that her son was becoming a little temperamental and difficult. She supposed that it was just a *phase* which, rather to her surprise, he suffered as much as a daughter would have done.

'I was about thirteen or fourteen,' she told Tom. 'Girls of course do, unless they're anaemic.'

'So you have reminded me before, darling.'

'Yes. Perhaps Sandy is a little under-developed, his voice broke rather late. I don't like to speak to him about his being cross if it's just physical.'

'I shouldn't worry. Wait until he goes up to Cambridge.'

'Oh dear, I do hope he'll be able to cope. I had a cousin who was sent down for—for getting involved with a girl in a gramophone shop.'

'Splendid.'

'Oh, Tom!'

But on the whole, she was not really apprehensive. Her husband had the most satisfactory way of disposing of her anxieties. Whenever possible he removed the weight of responsibility from her mind.

'I am so distressed at leaving you for the whole day,' she assured Sandy, when, wearing her best London clothes, she hugged him with unnecessary warmth before following Tom into the car.

'Have a good time,' said Sandy lugubriously.

'Of course I'm not really one for the theatre meself,' said

Mrs Bird, as she closed the hall door. 'Last time we went with the tickets Miss Chandler give us, we travelled up by bus which always gives me a headache, and Mr Bird couldn't hear the half of what they said on the stage and kept asking me what people were laughing at. I'd sooner stay at home and watch the telly myself. 'Course Susan liked it, being she's fond of the singing and that. You was away at school at the time so you wouldn't remember.'

Sandy made no reply. He was feeling ill-used and sorry for himself. Wandering into the morning room, he sat down on the window-seat and stared morosely at the leaf-strewn garden.

'If I was you I'd go out for a bit after you've had your dinner,' said Mrs Bird, following him. 'I daresay the sun 'ud do you good. You don't want to go too far, just along by the common and back by the farm. That shouldn't be too much for you, and it'd give you a nice appetite for tea.'

'It looks like rain,' said Sandy.

'Get along with you!' retorted Mrs Bird kindly. 'It looks a lot more settled than it was earlier on. What is it, don't you want to go by yourself?'

'It's so boring.'

'Well you're a funny one, you're usually on about never having any time on your own at school. Look, I tell you what, I'll get Susan to go with you if you like. She's done a good morning's work with me, and it won't hurt her to have a bit of a change. She's off tomorrow to spend a few days with her auntie. I reckon she'll find things a bit different when she starts her training. Not that she's one to waste her time and never has been. I'll have a word with her anyway when you come back with me dinner-time. She won't mind, she likes a nice walk.'

Sandy realizing that there was nothing more to be said, took up an illustrated magazine and exchanged the window-seat for a deep armchair. He glanced at the smooth photographs of beautiful country houses and splendid estates; they failed to arouse his interest and, for some reason he found inexplicable, he remembered the highly coloured plates the other chaps had pored over in the study and their smothered laughter. There was nothing funny in his opinion about a nude girl with a pretty smile; he didn't want to giggle and keep turning to the page again as if to be reassured that she was still there. He liked looking at the photographs when nobody else was present and there were no sniggering comments. He enjoyed the secrecy and the illicit pleasure of thinking about it. He even felt slightly frightened as though he were successfully protesting against the bonds of correction, the threat of interference.

He was very silent during his luncheon with the Birds and a little snappy when he was pressed to eat more.

'Come on now,' said Mr Bird, 'if we're going to see you rowing in the Boat Race up at college in a year or two, you'll have to put on a lot more weight than what you are now. Have a bit more of this rabbit pie. It'll build you up nice and strong.'

'No, *thank* you,' repeated Sandy, becoming very pink.

'Leaving room for the treacle pudding, are you? Come on; why, my boys wouldn't think anything of eating twice what you do.'

'Don't worry him if he feels he's had enough,' reproved Mrs Bird, 'he knows his own stomach best.'

'Dad,' interposed Susan, 'when you were in the Navy did they give you plum duff? I read that somewhere, and I expect it was nice and filling.'

Sandy's colour slowly faded. He knew that once Mr Bird was questioned on any matter connected with The Senior Service he would hold forth until, in desperation, his wife stopped him. And presumably his daughter knew the risks too. Gratitude welled within his heart; he looked across the table at Susan and met the merriment in her pretty eyes; he realized that she was not being sorry for him, they were just sharing a joke. Cautiously he ventured on a small smile which slowly broadened into a grin. Mrs Bird was scooping the remains of the rabbit pie on to her plate, Mr Bird was, regrettably, chasing a sodden crust in the gravy. And suddenly he knew that he liked them very much. They were both absorbed and comfortably greedy. He knew where he was with them and, because of their lack of false values, he respected them.

'I reckon Miss Chandler will be glad to get back,' Mrs Bird was saying. 'I don't fancy they feed them, not up to much, in hotels out of the season. Tinned stuff likely as not, *and* charge for it . . . There now, I've just remembered I forgot to tell whoever it was rung up to speak to Miss Chandler that I wouldn't be in to take any messages for her today. I do hope it wasn't bad news. Still, she'll be back herself tomorrow, and I'll be glad of it.'

'You!' said Mr Bird, 'you worry yourself over nothing, given the chance.'

'You're not a mother,' retorted his wife, to which indisputable statement he could find no reply at all.

'Is it about those people's daughter not coming home?' asked Susan.

'He didn't say, and I reckon it *was* her father because he sounded in a state, and it's my belief she wasn't back else he wouldn't have rung off so sharp.'

'My father says the chap often gets pretty sozzled,' said Sandy, 'which must be rather awful for Elizabeth.'

'Who's Elizabeth?' demanded Mrs Bird suspiciously.

'The daughter,' explained Sandy, blushing furiously. 'She's frightfully sort of modern. My father told me to take her to the cinema once. She made me feel an awful ass. I think she's about my age but she dolls herself up terrifically and, of course, that makes her seem much older. I—I was terrifically bored, actually.'

'I reckon you was, and so should I have been,' said Mr Bird, with intent to be helpful. 'If I'd a daughter like that I'd scrub her face with Monkey Brand.'

'Don't talk so daft,' advised his wife, 'you don't catch anyone using that sort of thing nowadays, not even for floors. According to the telly, it's all creams and that, if they want to look like film stars . . . She wouldn't have told you, Mr Sandy, I don't suppose, if she'd friends she stays with overnight in London?'

'No, because she lives with her people in a flat near my father, and I think he said the night porter's on duty to let people in if he's warned they'll be late. I don't think my father likes Elizabeth's people much. Why do you want to know?'

'Mrs Bird,' explained Mr Bird, 'has got what you might call a hunch. There's been telephone calls the twice for Miss Chandler while she's been away and no name left. Putting two and two together, it looks to me as if the girl's gone missing.'

'Oh, I shouldn't think so,' said Sandy. 'I should imagine she's quite used to looking after herself. She may have had the outdoor key or something.'

'Perhaps she's had an accident,' said Susan. 'Everybody ought to carry an identity card or something because it's a help to the police. They said that at my First Aid lectures.'

'Of course the telephone calls might have been from anybody,' added Sandy, 'though it's a bit odd they didn't leave a message. If it was Elizabeth's father, he was probably feeling a bit the morning-after-the-night-before and wasn't coping awfully well, which would explain why he forgot to leave his name. Could you tell me what sort of voice it was, Mrs Bird?'

165

'I'd say sort of husky and a bit thick; quite like a gentleman's.'

'I shouldn't worry, honestly. She's probably turned up by now,' said Sandy.

'I don't think she ought to make her mother anxious,' Susan told him.

'Of course she didn't ought to,' agreed Mr Bird, 'but when there's a lot of this bridge playing and that going on, it gets a hold on some, like bingo, and they don't seem able to stop, no matter whether they've children or not. You can't really blame the girl for feeling she doesn't matter.'

'Well, as I say, I'll be glad when tomorrow comes,' declared Mrs Bird, 'and Miss Chandler gets back to take her own calls. I daresay she'll hear some news quick enough if there's any trouble, and she'd tell me when I come to work if I ask her. It 'ud set my mind at rest, I know that. I can't help thinking what might have happened.'

'Yes, well, you take an aspirin tonight,' advised Mr Bird, 'and forget it. I'll be glad to have a bit of peace meself without you thrashing about like you did last night.'

'Poor old Mum,' said Susan, affectionately.

' 'Course nothing is said about poor old Dad,' said her father, and winked at Sandy. 'Never trouble that *I* was kep' awake till all hours. When you're a family man, Mr Sandy, don't you let yourself be put upon. Bear me in mind; I'm an object lesson, I am.'

'I haven't actually observed any evidence of your being excessively ill-treated,' said Sandy, doing his best, and was much encouraged by Mrs Bird's approving nod.

'Nice to know someone's got a bit of sense,' she said, 'he doesn't know where he's well off, does he, Mr Sandy? Dear-oh-dear, what I have to put up with!' and bestowing her severe smile upon her unabashed husband, she told Susan to clear the table. 'You sit still and rest your hand,' she told their guest, 'the swelling's not down yet, is it, Susan?'

'It's getting better.'

'It hardly hurts at all now,' he told them. He was very happy; at school the Sanatorium had been full of influenza cases and the staff had been glad to get rid of him. 'My go only lasted 48 hours,' he told Susan, as they walked out into the windy sunshine.

'Are they kind to you in there?'

'Oh, yes. Of course they get pretty rushed if there are a lot of chaps all laid up at one time.'

'Shall you be sorry to be leaving your school?'

'Not really . . . Well, perhaps, in a way. It's difficult to say really.'

'I expect you're kind of used to it, even if you don't like it all that,' she suggested.

'Yes,' said Sandy, 'that's just about sums it up.'

'I reckon that's the way most of us feel when we're faced with a big change. One's just got to face up to it, I suppose. I keep wondering what it'll be like working in a hospital away from home, but I'm sure I'll soon get used to it. And it'll be nice nursing little children.'

'They'll be lucky to have you,' said Sandy. Walking beside her, up the long chalky path which led to the brown ploughed field, he felt unexpectedly happy. 'Be careful how you go,' he said, as the track grew narrow, 'there are an awful lot of loose stones about after the rain.'

'When we were children we used to cycle down to see how fast we could go, my brothers an' me,' she told him. 'I wonder we never came off. But you don't think of that sort of thing when you're young. I suppose it's only natural.'

'Yes,' said Sandy, and wished that he could match their intrepidity with his own.

'I don't suppose we had much imagination,' she said.

'That's better than having too much,' he assured her.

'Like me, for instance.'

'Have you?' she said. 'Perhaps it's because you're not very strong.'

'I expect so,' he answered. He thought it very nice of her to be so sympathetic. The path between the hedges had grown narrow and the rough chalky ground made their steps uneven. He wished that his right arm was not bandaged. 'Go carefully,' he said.

'I will do. You mind yourself.'

'Yes. We'll be over the worst part in a minute or two . . . look out, you nearly tripped then . . . would you mind if I held your hand, just till we get over this bit? . . .'

Her warm fingers, a little roughened, lay confidently under his. 'I don't really walk very much,' he said. 'My step-father is very keen on fishing and often takes me with him : and we go out in the car quite a lot.' For some reason he felt he had to go on talking.

The stoney path had given way to a wider sandy track leading to a stile and the ploughed fields. He wondered whether he ought to loosen his hold on her small fingers. Her quietness made him feel shy. 'I think it's frightfully plucky of you to take up nursing,' he said. 'I should imagine it's a pretty hard life.'

She withdrew her hand very gently from his. They had come to the stile and the path between the bare fields. The rising wind had grown colder, ruffling Sandy's hair and bringing soft colour to Susan's little face.

'I think,' she said, 'we'd best hurry on before the rain comes down.'

He lifted the gate's chain and, letting her through, paused to see her waiting for him. Tentatively he put out his un-injured hand and, drawing her closer, bent to kiss her fresh cheek.

'Thank you,' he said, but what he was thanking her for he hardly knew.

'We'd best get back,' she repeated.

Walking beside her, he was aware of a curious kind of elation. She was not annoyed with him or in any way distressed, nor did it seem to him that she was used to being kissed. It was something natural which had happened and which they would share with no one; it possessed no danger and led to no future.

This evening he would be gone and soon her work would claim her, and he in his turn would begin another education. Everything was a fresh beginning. His worries seemed to have subsided and the surface of his mind to have become smooth. He had a sense of emancipation, not abrupt but releasing him from the imprisonment of childish affections. He was not startled because in some inexplicable way he seemed to find his freedom familiar : it was as though he had known it all before, just as her soft cheek beneath his shy kiss had stilled the protests of his questing heart.

'I fancy,' she was saying, 'the rain'll hold off just long enough for us to get back dry. My Dad will be wild if he doesn't get all his potatoes in before it comes down again. He takes ever such a pride in his vegetables.'

'I know,' said Sandy. 'It would infuriate him to see what the cooks at school can do to an honest cabbage.'

'It's a shame to waste good food,' she assured him.

He was glad when they got back to the warm kitchen and the comfortable smell of toasted bread. Mrs Bird placed a large freshly baked fruit cake in the middle of the table.

'I hope you've brought a good appetite back from your walk, Mr Sandy,' she said. 'Mr Bird's gone off to his bell-ringing practice but he'll be back in plenty time for his tea.'

'Aren't we going to wait for him?'

169

F*

'He doesn't have more than the one cup till six o'clock when we have our meal,' explained Mrs Bird, warming the brown teapot, 'fish or cheese pie, or fried egg and chips, or a nice bit of boiled ham; he always eats well, I will say that for him. He never has been one to peck at his food.'

Sandy wondered if this was a little slap at him, but he felt too contented to care. He sat in the comfortable basket chair beside the crackling wood fire and watched Susan buttering the toasted bread and piling the square little slices into the pink china dish with the fluted cover. He wondered if she would grow up to look like her mother, and become plump and shapeless, with her rosy face a little raddled and her round chin doubled. He wondered, too, if she would always be amiable and kind.

He was not sure why but somehow he felt rather critical and a little superior now. He wished that he might go home and not wait to be fetched by Tom, that he could be quiet and read his book or even do nothing at all, but loll on the sofa and know again his newly found independence.

'Tired after your walk, Mr Sandy? How's your wrist feeling?'

'It hardly hurts at all now, thanks.' He wanted to belong to himself, to be grateful to no one, to hug to himself his liberty.

'I daresay you'd like the telly on for the news, Mr Sandy.'

He felt that there was no conspiracy between himself and Susan, she neither sought his attention nor ignored it; she was quiet, open, and friendly. He felt a sense of relief and no disappointment. Their secret remained trivial and inviolate. What did matter was his own sensation of a gained individuality. He had achieved a measure of escape. Neither his mother nor Tom would know anything about it : to the one it might be a source of anxiety, to the other a joke.

But there was no risk of either happening : he would

keep his own counsel and its significance would dwindle that his own self-importance might gain. He knew that he loved Milly no less, but the pressure of a world outside that which he had known before, became a stronger reality. He no longer cherished a sense of dependence, he maintained a privacy which added to his stature.

'Well, they're back quick,' said Mrs Bird, as eventually Tom Garland tapped at the cottage door. 'Before there was cars they used to call it a Sabbath's day's journey to London.'

Susan came out to see him off. 'I hope your wrist gets well soon,' she said.

'I hope you have a nice time with your aunt,' said Sandy.

'Oh, she will do,' said Mrs Bird, 'her cousins will keep her lively. How was the weather up in London, Mr Garland?'

'Ghastly,' said Tom cheerfully. 'Come along, old chap.'

'Thanks awfully for having me,' said Sandy.

'It's a pleasure,' returned Mrs Bird politely.

'Well, darling,' said Milly, as Sandy joined her in the car, 'you looked tired. You must have a good rest before dinner. Has it seemed a very long day?'

He was not sure; of one thing only he was certain, he had become somehow different, a person in his own right. He was out of the net of protection, the loved and resented care of childhood. He felt disgruntled, despising everyone, his mother for her reluctance to loosen her hold, Susan for the simplicity of her understanding, and, above all, himself for his growing sense of anticlimax. He wanted to retain a pleasure which was fast diminishing.

'I'm on my own,' he muttered, when he reached his room, but there was really nothing particularly remarkable in that. And his confusion mounted. 'She didn't appear to like it,' he told himself, 'my kissing her, I mean. She didn't try to kiss *me* or anything. Well, actually I don't think it made any impression on her at all. Probably that's quite a good thing. The whole business seems slightly pointless.'

He flung himself on his bed and closed his eyes and presently an agreeable melancholy possessed him. That, of course, was how he ought to feel, since no aspiring poets were ever content. It was important to be slightly unhappy and to avoid consolation. Sleepily he attempted to concentrate on the essential mood but it eluded him. Everything became intangible, unreal, elusive. He tried to recall each thought as it drifted through his mind but none would stay. Half-dreams lapped him about and drew him into the ease of forgetfulness. He pressed his face into his familiar pillow and slept.

Chapter Sixteen

'WHAT'S THE idea of going back so soon?'

'I only booked for a long week-end,' Caroline told him.

'Why not stay on?' Alex looked not at her but the whisky at the bottom of his glass.

'No, I must get back. For one thing I'm baby-sitting this evening.'

'Surely they can get someone else.' His query was perfunctory rather than persuasive. She knew him well enough to realize that on the whole he would rather that she did not stay, but at the same time her presence was a sort of insurance lest he should need her.

'They could of course ask one of their friends, but Rosie's used to me, and she doesn't mind her people leaving her for a few hours if I'm there.'

'Spoilt brat,' he said, but she detected the relief in his voice. He was probably feeling well and therefore her presence was superfluous. 'What time are you going?'

'Directly after lunch.'

'If this blasted weather goes on I shall probably leave here myself and go back to London at the end of the week.'

'It may suddenly get warmer, in which case it would do you more good to stay on.'

'I doubt it.' He looked a little secretive, a little amused. The hotel lounge was empty, all the elderly residents were upstairs in their bedrooms resting from the exhaustion of having nothing to do.

'What an extraordinary life it must be,' she said.

'Here d'you mean? Oh, I don't know, I suppose it suits them. I imagine you'd hate it.'

'I'd rather be dead.'

He looked startled. Her quietness was more convincing than any emphasis would have been.

'Well, it's not the only alternative to your present existence. Have you thought any more about our joining forces?'

'No.'

'Well you ought to.' But there was no urgency in his statement.

She almost wished that she had the courage to show him the affront of her understanding. She knew that once again the temporary obsession held him in thrall. In the forefront of his mind was the girl in the flower shop with her automatic charm, her youthful beauty, her sweet mischief.

Caroline looked away from him in unexpected pity. What she loved in him was not anything to commend itself to a girl, who would merely observe a tired old man, practising his worn tricks to no purpose; in unconscious cruelty she would parade the riches of her youth, and think no more of it.

Caroline's heart ached. She did not want him to suffer : if he were unkind she could accept it, if he were imperceptive she could ignore it, if long years ago she had given him her whole heart and paid the penalty of a senseless devotion, she could endure it.

But she was too old now to suffer any more indignity. She knew that she could not join her life to his and accept its consequences. All that she had had to offer she gave, a loyalty and a love beyond his appreciation. All that she had to rely on was her own constancy. Pain had been her recur-

174

ring enemy for so long that its emergence failed to take her by surprise. But her distress was inescapable. That Alex had hurt her once again seemed less important than the fact that she despised herself for defending him in her mind. He was like that and there was nothing more to be said. Shoddy behaviour towards the end of a long life given to self-indulgence might be deplorable, but it was in keeping with his character. She understood that he frequently needed her consideration, her protection when he became ill, her readiness not to obstruct him when he went his own way. Had she seen him less clearly she might have hoodwinked herself into believing that he had not tarnished their relationship, but she could not commit so blatant an untruth before her own secret tribunal.

She was ashamed, not of him but of herself for lowering a standard to admit excuses. Yet to be reasonable seemed absurd. She was not influenced by self-justification or impressed by a desire to see herself as either wise or courageous. She had lived too long with disillusionment and with an unbroken devotion to dwell very securely with heroics. Conflicting emotions had wrenched her apart in the past but now she was too tired to risk their destruction. There were repairs to be done to each day's fair wear and tear, and more than that she was unwilling to face.

'I don't know why you can't wait until I clear off myself,' Alex was saying, 'it would be a perfectly simple matter for you to ring up and put off your baby-sitting nonsense.'

'I don't like letting people down for no good reason.'

'Aren't I a sufficiently good reason?'

She had an idea that he was trying to convince himself that he was being considerate, but she knew that he would be very disappointed if she suddenly changed her mind and said that she would stay. She even felt a wry amusement to think how inconvenient it would be for him to put off the plan he no doubt had made to renew his acquaintance with the little florist.

'Rosie's parents need to go out together and enjoy themselves sometimes,' she told him. 'It's one of the things that keeps their marriage together.'

'Why should you care?'

'Why not?'

'I thought she was having another child.'

'She is.'

'Milly more or less disappeared from public view for months before Sandy was born.'

'That's some while ago,' Caroline reminded him. 'Nowadays the sensible ones go about more or less as usual until their time's up.'

'Milly was always a fool. Pity you didn't marry me.'

'You don't really think that.'

'You appear to be in a slightly argumentative mood,' he told her, but he looked good humoured.

'I'm sorry, Alex, I'm a little tired.'

'Pity, I was hoping we could go for a short stroll before tea.'

'It's too cold.'

'You're not feeling ill, are you?'

'No, just a little weary. I don't always sleep awfully well.'

'Haven't you got something for that?'

'No, I don't bother. One doesn't expect at my age to sleep the night through.'

'Have you got a good doctor?'

'Yes, but I practically never see him. Doctors are for sick people, not for fusspots.'

'You are all right though really, aren't you, Caroline?'

'Yes, of course I am.'

'I know,' he said, 'that some people do find it rather trying on the coast when the wind's in the east. As I said before, you're too thin. And I wish you weren't. It worries me.'

'You mustn't let it.'

'Well, damn it all, of course it does. What do you take me for?' His face changed and he looked angry. 'Do you realize the trouble with you, Caroline? You know me too well.'

It was not the retort that she had expected. Once colour would have rushed to her face, now no easier relief came, her breath grew short and a little difficult. She was quiet until she felt she could answer him steadily. 'You think it a handicap?'

'You've always got an answer, haven't you? Look here, this is ridiculous, why should we quarrel? Don't spoil your last evening. If you insist on going, that is... What's that smile supposed to mean?'

'Was I smiling? I'm sorry, I didn't know.' She was too tired to fence with him, to assure him that she knew he could do very well without her for the next few days. She knew, too, that he felt a curious kind of pity for her because he was unkind and she made no effort to resist it. In a confused sort of way he understood that it was not sufficiently important to her any more, and he wished that it were. He had to exercise his own will and please himself, but his satisfaction was lessened if he were deprived of the ultimate pleasure of showing his superiority. He was incapable of knowing that she could accept the penalty of loving but not the burden of her own preservation.

'What time do you want to push off tomorrow?' he asked her.

'I've ordered the car for eleven.'

'Why not after lunch?'

'I don't like rushing and that will give me more time at home to arrange my day comfortably and possibly have a rest before I'm fetched to go over and look after Rosie.'

'Why the hell should it be you?'

'Why not? I happen to enjoy it. She likes being read to and she doesn't get enough of it in the ordinary way. Too many modern parents leave it to television to keep their children quiet whether what's on the screen is suitable or not.'

'Perhaps they know better than you do.'

'Sometimes but not always.'

'Why assume that you're the best judge?'

'Largely because it's a matter of instinct. Alex, this isn't the sort of thing we'll ever agree on, can't we drop it?'

'You always say that when you're getting the worst of an argument. All right, have it your own way. Anyhow, the whole thing's entirely unimportant . . . What's the matter, have you got a headache or something?'

'No.'

'I don't believe you. You look rotten. Caroline, will you make me a promise?'

'What about?'

'I want you to make an appointment to see your doctor and arrange with him to give you a complete overhaul.'

'Why on earth should I do that?'

'Because I'm worried about you.'

'Then you needn't be. Besides we mustn't swop rôles. It's really rather ridiculous, Alex.'

'I don't agree with you.' But he sounded uncertain. 'You don't think you're getting 'flu or anything?'

'I wouldn't be so tactless.'

'What? I do wish you'd get out of the habit of mumbling. I told you before : it's very irritating.'

'I'm sorry.'

'You've got an unfortunate habit of always putting me in the wrong. Good heavens, I wasn't asking you to apologise.

What's the *matter*, Caroline?'

'Nothing. Why, what have I said?'

'That's the whole trouble, you don't say anything. You carry self-control to the most unreasonable limits. *I* don't know what you're annoyed about : it's obscure to me. You never used to be like this. I've always thought that you were rather exceptionally sweet-tempered.'

'And now you've changed your mind.'

'Damn it all, Caroline, don't put words into my mouth. I don't know what all this is about, it's completely untypical. I suppose something's upset you. Why not tell me? We're supposed to be fond of each other, aren't we?'

She lay back in the stiff hotel armchair. The room seemed a prison and he her jailer. She wanted to escape from the weight of his presence. He overwhelmed her by the insistence of his complaints.

'You're frightened of something,' he said, and his tone changed. 'Look here, I didn't mean to upset you. If you feel you've really got to go back tomorrow, that's all right. I know you never like letting people down. I'm sorry if I seemed to be unfair.'

She hoped that he would soon cease to excuse his ill-temper. She knew that because he was looking forward to tomorrow's encounter, he could afford to exhibit magnanimity.

'I'll come over to see you when I get back next week,' he said.

'Don't you think you ought to stay a little longer to—to complete the cure?'

He gave her a quick glance of suspicion but she looked at him so quietly that he was, as she knew he would be, at once disarmed. Impossible for him to imagine that she was deliberately offering him exactly what he wanted. He did not want to acknowledge the wounds of her understanding.

179

In his own satisfaction he had to accept the deceits of compassion.

'We must have a long uninterrupted talk,' he said, 'at your place when I get back and I shall have the extreme satisfaction of disposing of all your arguments.'

She closed her eyes for a moment but whether in protest or because she was so tired he was unsure.

'Tell them,' he said, 'to send some tea up to your room and have a good rest before dinner.'

She agreed at once. The illusion of taking care of her chased all vexation from his face. It would prove a short-lived pleasure exactly suited to his present mood.

'And when I get back,' he said, 'we must go into this business of looking for somewhere to live.' And added, with a little less assurance : 'You'd like that, wouldn't you?'

'It sounds lovely.'

'I thought you'd think that. Now you go along and get your shut-eye.'

He was almost jocular but she was not certain that he was not slightly nervous as well. She got up slowly and straightened her back. All that she wanted now was the solace of her own company.

Chapter Seventeen

'WELL, IF you ask me, I think she got off a lot luckier than she deserved,' said the night porter.

'You *could* say that,' replied the day porter, 'since she's still alive, but seeing she had to get herself out of the car away from the bloke, and run slap-wallop into a lorry, I reckon it wasn't too funny. What happened to the chap?'

'Catch him hanging around! He made off pronto, and left everyone else to clear up the mess. Somebody took his number, but the police say it was a stolen car, found abandoned that night in Clapham. I doubt they'll ever catch up on him. They asked her father if she was in the habit of thumbing lifts from strangers, which I don't fancy he liked, and her mother who was on the brink of a fit of the high-strikes, swore her daughter'd never do such a thing. Good as gold she was, of *course*. I wouldn't care to go into the witness box and swear to that meself; rotten little bitch she is, to my way of thinking.'

'They'll do anything for a giggle nowadays,' declared the younger porter, 'as I said before it's not her I blame, it's her parents. They should be ashamed of themselves, not troubling to bring her up proper. I reckon it's taught 'em a lesson this time.'

'I doubt it, some never learn. They say her neck's broke.'

'They can do a lot for that these days. She'll get over it. How about her face?'

'I fancy it was mostly cuts. Luckily he didn't go for her in the middle of Epping Forest or somewhere, else she might have been murdered or worse. I fancy she'll have to stay in hospital a tidy time. Fat lot of good education does when they're like that. Well, I'm off to m'breakfast, an' if I'm wanted I'm off duty, and nothing's goin' to interfere with that, never mind what they're after.'

The young day porter nodded and went off to the broom cupboard, subduing an inclination to whistle. Last evening he had been to the pictures with his girl and, blissfully sucking peppermint toffees, had watched the screen, gazing at scenes of violence with guns, scenes of sex in luxurious beds, and shattering musical noises optimistically calculated to arouse passion; it was all plush seat entertainment.

'It don't seem right to me,' said the young porter's girl friend, 'not to behave so rough.'

'They have to give us a bit of all sorts,' he told her. 'You don't need to watch if you'd sooner not, duckie. I reckon the Muppets is more in your line! To tell you the truth, I like something to make me laugh, meself. There's plenty of the other thing in this bad old world without goin' out to look for it.'

'That's just what I think.'

'Ah well, we're clever, you see. Pity there isn't more like us. Have another toffee.'

'Ta. How's the girl at the flats getting on? I forgot to ask you.'

'Not too good, but she'll get over it.'

'Poor thing! She must have been ever so frightened.'

'Oh, she's tough, don't you worry. Been brought up all wrong. Doesn't give a damn for anyone but herself.'

'I think it's very sad. I don't see how they can get on without they love somebody.'

'You've said a mouthful,' he assured her. 'It strikes me there's a lot of good sense in that little napper of yours.'

Mrs Bird in her snug cottage, shook her head and looked more than usually severe. 'So that's what they kept telephoning from London about, though how Miss Chandler could have helped them to find her, I don't know. It's not likely she'd have known anything. Still, I suppose they thought any port in a storm.'

'There's not much sense in saying that,' returned Mr Bird, 'it don't mean anything.'

'It means,' retorted his wife, 'she'd have helped if she could have. And don't keep on arguing about it. She rung up London directly she come back, which she didn't have to have done, and of course them up there had to tell her the whole story. I don't say I'm not sorry for the girl because I am, but she must have known better than to go off with a stranger . . .'

'I reckon he enticed her,' said Mr Bird darkly. 'Might have taken her to a pub and put something in her drink.'

'Girls in her class haven't any business to take up with strangers,' declared Mrs Bird. 'Come to that, not in any class if they've a ha-penny worth of sense. As I've said to Susan time after time, never mind if they're kerb crawling and stopping to ask the time or the way, don't answer, just keep walking straight on.'

'You don't have to tell her more than the once,' said Mr Bird, 'and seeing we don't let her out alone in lonely parts after dark, there's no call to keep on about it.'

'It wasn't in lonely parts,' persisted Mrs Bird, 'it was London, which makes it worse. When I went over to Miss Chandler this morning she told me young Mr Sandy had rung her up and told her about it. You know what boys are like, anything for a bit of excitement, though to give him his due, he's a quiet enough lad. He says his father's coming back from the sea earlier than expected. Well, all I can say, I hope he stops up in London and doesn't come troubling Miss Chandler down here. She don't look too well to me.'

'No one with a bit of sense would go to the sea in weather like this,' said Mr Bird, with contempt. 'It don't do you a bit of good, not with the wind in the east and all. I should know bein' I'd spent half me life with it. I'd sooner stop in m' own home, by m' own fireside nowadays than believe all them adverts about us being as good as the South of France where you can't even order yourself a glass of Bass without 'em jabbering a lot of nonsense in a foreign language at you.'

'Well, if you don't know what they're saying, I don't see how you can tell it's nonsense. Still you haven't got to go over there so you needn't keep on about it.'

'What are you getting your coat on for,' interrupted Mr Bird, 'you're not going back to Miss Chandler's this evening are you?'

'Just for a few minutes. I want to give her her supper in bed and see her tucked up comfortable. She had that little madam Rosie to mind all last evening, and of course them precious parents of hers wasn't home till after midnight, never mind they'd promised to be back early. 'Course they drove her home, but, though it's not more than a step, I was glad to know this morning they got her back safe, seeing as like as not they was what some call "very nicely thank you!" Seems a silly way of putting it if you ask me.'

'What they mean is,' explained Mr Bird, 'that they've had a skinful. Speaking for meself I don't think it's right, not when there's young children in the home. I wonder at Miss Chandler encouraging 'em.'

'She doesn't,' contradicted his wife. 'It's her policy to live and let live, and though I don't say I hold with it meself, I reckon she's as much entitled to her own opinion as the rest of us. What I *don't* like is her looking so done in these days.'

'Well, she's no chicken, you know.'

'She may not be, but that's not to say she's got to look as if she doesn't care what happens to her. I wouldn't have thought Miss Chandler 'ud give up so easy. She's not one to show her feelings, but since she come back from her week-end at the sea she's got me worried.'

'Then why don't you get her to call the doctor?'

'She wouldn't do that,' retorted Mrs Bird, 'unless she was real bad. If you ask me it's not a case for tonics and that. Real sad she looks if you happen to catch her when she doesn't know you're watching.'

'Well, I don't see what good you're going to do going over there again, when like as not she'll have locked up and turned in. Maybe she feels she can do with a good long night.'

'She may do but I'd feel a bit easier in my mind if I saw she was all right.'

'You know what you are,' grumbled Mr Bird, drawing on his wellingtons, 'you're an old fusspot.'

'You haven't got to come, it won't take me a few moments on m' bike.'

'I daresay not. Get your coat on and don't argufy. You're not goin' on your own an' that's that.'

'You're not a bad old stick,' said Mrs Bird, and dealt him an affectionate buffet, 'pity's there's not more of your sort around . . . here, stand out of my light can't you, clumsy! How can I get to my kitchen with you blocking up the whole place?'

Caroline switched on the porch light and drew back the bolts. 'Who's there?'

'Only us, Miss,' said Mrs Bird.

'Is anything the matter? I'm just going to bed.'

'The wife,' explained Mr Bird, 'had a fancy you wasn't feelin' too well. We've brought you a drop of hot soup and a bit of creamed chicken.'

'That sounds lovely. I wasn't going to bother about any supper. Come into the sitting-room : it's still warm in there.'

'Pardon me, Miss,' interrupted Mrs Bird, 'you go along and have a hot bath and mind you don't stop in it long on account of it being weakening. I'll bring your tray up to you once you're in bed. Mr Bird can sit and watch the football if you've no objection.'

'You must both have a glass of sherry. It's very sweet of you to spoil me.'

'Yes, well, you make haste and get your bath and hurry off to bed. I'll pop your hot water bottle in. I know some are always cracking off about electric blankets stopping hot longer, but I don't hold with them. I'd sooner have what I'm used to. You know where you are then. I've known funny things happen with blankets in the bed.'

'Or without 'em,' murmured Mr Bird, and was rapidly nudged into silence as usual by his wife.

Caroline, however, smiled at him and paused to unlock the cellarette. 'Help yourselves to the sherry,' she said. 'By the way, I've got young Sandy Orme coming to spend the night tomorrow. His nice feckless mother forgot that he's breaking up in the morning, and that she and her husband will be away till the following evening. She thought, very naturally, that he'd hate coming back to a cold empty house, so of course I agreed to fetch him at the station and bring him here. His poor mother was full of apologies.'

'As well she might be,' declared Mrs Bird, 'putting it all on you ! Has Mr Sandy left school for good then? I reckon it's about time that young man grew up a bit. It don't do to be so dependent on others.'

'A spell in the Navy wouldn't have done him no harm,' said Mr Bird. 'He's a nice enough lad, and speaks very polite, but he'll have to stand on his own feet one day and the sooner the better.'

'I like him,' said Caroline, and her decision caused the Birds to become silent. 'If he's taking his time to mature, he may be none the worse for that. I'm very much inclined to think that he's got a mind of his own. Well, I must go and get that bath of mine.'

'That's funny, you know,' said Mr Bird, as Caroline left them. 'I wouldn't have thought she'd have troubled to stand up for him, not like that.'

'Maybe she didn't care about him being criticized. Or else she's sorry for the boy. I daresay she's got her reasons. It's not as though she's got any call to think much of his father.'

'*Him!*' snorted Mr Bird. 'The less said about that the better. I dunno what his mother could have been thinking about marrying him in the first place.'

'Well, there's no accounting for these things. It takes all sorts to make a world, good *and* bad. I sometimes wonder . . .'

'What?'

'Nothing.'

'You must have meant something when you started to speak.'

'Not really . . . of course she's always stood up for him . . . that time he went after Susan, she wouldn't hear a word.'

'Who wouldn't for goodness sake?' complained Mr Bird.

'Miss Chandler.'

'What's she got to do with it? We wasn't speaking to her, was we? I believe you're half asleep, it's about time we went home.'

Mrs Bird looked at the untouched sherry in her glass. 'You can have it if you like,' she said, 'I'd sooner have a good cup of tea myself. I'll take her supper up now.'

'I was,' said Alex, 'very worried about you. You looked rotten.'

'Did I? I'm sorry.'

'Why say it like that? Don't you believe me?'

'As much as you would expect me to.'

'What's the point of being so sceptical? I was genuinely concerned. As a matter of fact, if you must know, I thought you looked appallingly unhappy. Were you, Caroline?'

'No. I just happened to feel a little too exhausted to convince myself that I could take very much more.'

'Why in the world,' he protested, 'should you imagine there was anything more to *take* as you call it?' But meeting her direct glance, he looked angry. 'Why let it upset you? . . . All right, you needn't tell me. Look here, to put the record straight, I went back to that damned florist, for no better reason, I suppose, than that I was bored. Whereupon I discovered the bird had flown, having telephoned that morning to say she was not returning. So I expended a pound or two on the tulips you see over there, commiserated with the shop owners on their loss and decided that it was time I returned to London. Which I did, telephoned to you, and came down today. Incidentally your visit to the sea, in spite of everything, seems to have done you good after all. You look astonishingly well.'

'I feel it.'

'What a comfortable woman you are! And absurdly lovable.'

'Why that?'

'Only you can tell me. Will you marry me, Caroline?'

'No, dear Alex, for the third and last time, no.'

'Tell me why. I make you happy, don't I?'

'Yes.'

'Well then, I could make you happier.'

'No, this is the only possible way.'

'Does that mean because you don't love me enough?'

'I shall always love you, Alex. More than anything in the world.'

'Then I don't understand. Is it because I don't toe the line, because you can't take my way of loving you?'

'No. But I don't want to try to explain. I need you as you are, that's really all that matters. I couldn't bear to lose you.'

'You never will.'